TRUST AND BELIEVE

Dedicated to my mom, Gwendolyn Loban... *May you rest in peace.*

Richard C. Loban

PROLOGUE

I lost my breath. I struggled and fought for air with each gasp. My sense of hearing vanished. It was like all of a sudden someone hit the mute button. My eyes were wide open and glassy. I stared up at the big blue sky, hoping to see my Lord and Savior charge through the clouds on his big white horse, ready to come and save me; but he never came.

A few onlookers stood by and watched unsympathetically as the EMT's scrambled to keep me alive. They knew they were losing me. My vision was starting to fade. Everything became blurry, and in an instant went black…

Am I gone?

That's the dream that jerked me out of my sleep every morning for the past 10 years, but this morning was different. There was no screaming, no sweating, and no cell mate with the smell of fish on her breath to ask if I was alright.

I'm going home today. After a decade in this bitch I'm going home, and It's such a crazy feeling.

Imagine yourself traveling on a high speed train through a long tunnel. You look out the window and only see your reflection. Everything is dark but you know you're moving. You can feel yourself moving. You're not in a rush to get to your destination but you know that it's coming, and when the end is near and your ride is over, you wish you had more time to reflect. That's how this bid felt.

I missed out on a lot over the years, but I can't say that I regret doing what I did to land me here. To me it was just a small drop in the bucket compared to what was done to my son. He won't get a second chance, and I wish that I could have made everyone involved pay.

My mom, the voice of reason, picked me up from the prison, and made it her business to be my support base as I reacclimate back into society. She left behind everything and everyone she knew, in order to relocate to the east coast after I was convicted. She never missed a visit, she wrote letters, and kept money in my commissary for the entire duration of my bid. I felt so guilty. Not because of what I put her through, but because I wasn't able to finish what I started.

It's a long ride from upstate New York back down to the boroughs; and where they had me at, I was damn near a stones throw away from Canada. During the ride, the conversation was kept to a minimum; we mostly listened to the radio on the trip down.

A picture of my son and I was taped to the dashboard of my mom's car, and I did nothing but stare at it the entire ride home. He had to be around 7 or 8 years old in the picture, but the look he had on his face, told his life story.

And what a story it was...

1 "AGE DOES NOT PROTECT YOU FROM LOVE. BUT LOVE, TO SOME EXTENT, PROTECTS YOU FROM AGE."

- JEANNE MOREAU

I was born in the spring of 1985, to the not so proud parents of Charlene Riley, and Ivan Borisov. I was given the name Robert, after my mother's father, whom I never met due to him being killed in Vietnam. Robert Richard Riley's my name; don't wear it out, the illegitimate child of Charlene. My father Ivan, a Russian gymnast who defected during the 1984 Olympics, must have really wanted him some brown sugar, cause he wasted little time running up in my mom only two days after he met her. He was either over persistent, or my mom was simply that easy; you decide. If you let her tell it, she claimed that Ivan came to the concession stand where she worked, and damn near broke his neck trying to talk to her; bad English and all. Well I guess his persistence paid off, because nine months later here I am. A half black, half white, little terror that looks Mexican.

My mom was color struck. Every man she ever dated was fair skinned. They had to be White, Latino, or "high yellow" Black, for her to give them some play. She on the other hand, was dark as tar, with heavy African features. The old slave masters didn't infiltrate her bloodline at all. She absolutely hated her complexion, but I always thought she was beautiful.

My father though, was "deathly" pale. He was white as a ghost, and had a short muscular build. I would visit him from time to time, but it became few and far in between once my mom picked up and moved to New York.

Los Angeles was where we were originally from, and I loved it there. It didn't matter that the area where we lived was super violent, it will always be home to me. All my friends were there, my Grand mama was there, my whole entire world was right there.

I hated that my mom all of a sudden out of the blue, packed everything up, and moved us just before my seventh birthday.

She took me from the warm sunshine and the smell of fresh gun powder, to the freezing cold winter and the crazy rat infestation of New York.

In L A, we lived with my grandma in a small house right off Crenshaw. It wasn't nothing to brag about, just a nice little well kept bungalow.

In New York, we lived in a small run down apartment in the Bronx, along with my mom's new truck driving, Puerto Rican boyfriend Manuel. She met him when he was passing through our town making one of his deliveries.

Again, it was another world wind relationship she got caught up in, that made her uproot us, and move all the way across the country.

My grandma was highly upset about it. She couldn't believe that my mom would follow behind some guy she hardly knew. But that's how my mom is; real impulsive. She don't think about shit; she just does.

Manuel was cool though. I could barely

understand him, but he was cool. His English was awful for someone who was born in this country; you would have thought he just got off the boat. I definitely wanted to attend the same schools he went to. Imagine the mischief I could get away with there. Evidently they don't pay much attention to their students. I probably could get away with murder. - Literally!

The elementary school I wound up going to was P.S. 154, in the Mott Haven section of the Bronx. I pretty much adapted to my new surroundings even though it took me a while to get use to the crowded classroom. It was packed wall to wall with black and Hispanic kids. All of us poor, and basically that's the only thing we had in common. The teacher was an older white woman named Mrs. Ford, who was there to just ride out the year until her retirement. She just scribbled some stuff on the board, handed us a worksheet to practice our handwriting, and we were on our own. The classroom was noisy. The majority of the kids spent the day laughing, talking, and running around throwing things at each other. I just quietly sat in the back of the class and observed. All the Hispanic kids were on one side of the room, and all the black kids on the other. I really didn't pay too much attention to it, until Mrs. Ford came to me and whispered,

"Why don't you sit on the other side of the room so you can be closer to your friends?"

"They ain't my friends," I said.

"Are you sure honey? I know you kids like to get together and speak that Spanish".

"I don't speak Spanish."

"Okay, shoot yourself," she uttered as she walked back to her desk.

This was something I had to deal with all my life. People mistaking me for a Hispanic, or an Arab person, rather than a light skinned black. But it had its benefits as well. Especially when It came to interacting with the Spanish chicks.

It wasn't long before I got into my first brush with the law. Yes, a seven year old in the first grade is about to get into some shit.

My temporary, common law step daddy, good 'old Manuel had a collection of weapons that he kept locked away in a safe in his bedroom closet. Every now and then he would pull a couple of guns out and clean them at the kitchen table. I would watch him intently. He would say, "No good for you Robby". That's what he called me, "Robby". I guess Robert was too hard for him to say. He would never let me touch the guns, and I think I made him very uncomfortable sitting there watching him clean them. He would say, "Go play Robby, Go play". I would get up and leave the table and pretend I was playing, but my eyes would be on him. I just wish somehow I could get into that safe. I wanted to get my hands on one of those guns.

Soon enough I got my chance when my mom, Charlene, wanted to put all her personal documents (birth certificates, tax papers, etc) in the safe just in case of a fire, and she hounded Manuel for the combination. He didn't want to give it to her; instead he said he would put the documents in the safe himself. But my mom said to Manuel, "What if you're not here and I need something out the safe? You be gone for weeks at a time. What I'm supposed to do?"

"Wait till I get back," Manuel replied.

"Fuck out of here Manuel. Wait till you get back? You're bugging."

"Yes wait till I get back. Everything will be ok"

This argument went on for like an hour, until Manuel caved in and gave her the combination. Now all I had to do was wait for my mom to slip up, and bam! I'll have my hands on some heat!

It didn't take long for that to happen. Charlene, running her mouth on the phone like usual, was putting stuff in the safe and didn't close the door back completely. So I quietly snuck into her bedroom, reached into the safe, grabbed the first gun I could get my hands on, and tossed it in my book bag.

Show and tell is gonna be a motherfucker tomorrow!

I always arrived at school on time. My mom would walk me there every day on her way to work. "Bye baby, behave in class today?" She would always say, as she planted a kiss on my cheek.

"Okay momma I will."

"Love you!"

"Love you too momma."

Then I'd take off running up the steps and through the schools main door.

Today was no different. After I made my way to class and took my seat on the "black" side of the room, I waited for everyone to settle down. Mrs. Ford proceeded with her normal routine of taking attendance, reciting the pledge of allegiance with the class, and handing out our daily worksheets. Soon as she began writing on the blackboard, is when I reached into my book bag, and pulled out the small but heavy handgun. I took aim on Mrs. Ford's flat wide ass. I had no rhyme or reason, I just thought it was a big enough target to hit. The snotty nose kid sitting next to me shouted, "ooohhh he got a guuun!"

Mrs. Ford turned around, scanned over the classroom, and caught me pointing the gun at her. She sternly said,

"Robert put that toy away. You'll have plenty of time to play during recess!"

At first I was taken aback a bit. I never heard Mrs. Ford raise her voice before. I know it's only been a month since school started, and I really didn't know her that well, but damn she startled me. I was about to put it away but that little voice inside of me said, 'Fuck that bitch. Shoot her in the ass.' And that's exactly what I did. When she turned back around and continued to write whatever she was writing on the board, I pulled the trigger... Boom!

The gun flew out of my hand, my ears were ringing, and my fellow classmates scattered. I saw Mrs. Ford grab her right ass cheek, and fall to the floor. The ringing in my ears started to be drowned out by the screams. Everyone in the classroom was screaming. School security rushed into the room, and before you knew it the police and EMT's were there. They whisked me off to the principals office where the cops began to question me. More like yell at me, than ask questions. I broke down and started to cry for my momma. I'm not ashamed to admit it. Remember, I was only seven years old. The principal told me that my mom was notified, and that she was on her way, but I needed to tell the police where I got the gun. Trying to be diplomatic he spoke softly and said,

"Son, where did you get the gun? Did you find it on the street? Did you bring it from home?"

I just sat there sniffling, swinging my feet back and forth in the chair, and steadily looked around the room for a friendly face. And there it was, my momma with all her ghetto fabulousness! Hair done up, lip gloss popping, nails did, with an attitude to match. She burst into the office screaming,

"Robert, what the hell they got you in here for? My baby didn't do nothing!"

"Ma'am, ma'am, please calm down. We're trying to conduct an investigation," an officer said.

"Investigate my ass. He's only seven years old and y'all in here ganging up on him. Robert, what they trying to say you did?"

"Ma'am, your son brought a gun to class and shot the teacher."

"Shot the teacher? Robert did you shoot your teacher?"~

She looked at one of the officers and asked,~

"Where'd he get the gun?"~

Then she turned to me.

"Robert, where'd you get the gun from?"

I shrugged. The room got real quiet for a moment and then my mom yelled out, "Manuel! He got the gun from my boyfriend Manuel!"

That's all the cops wanted to hear.

Charlene willingly let the cops come up in our crib, and even opened the safe for them. Every gun Manuel had in his stash was illegal. Serial numbers were scratched off, and the ones with serial numbers were reported stolen. Now all the heat was off of me and on him. They wanted him bad, but they had to wait. Manuel was out of state making his deliveries. He wouldn't be back until the end of the week.

I don't know If Charlene had some pent up anger against Manuel, or she simply was trying to protect me. Whatever the reason, she was being real extra with it. She told the cops that he loved to get high, and that he traveled back and forth to Miami a lot so he might be transporting drugs as well. Everything she said was a lie. She didn't even give him a heads up about anything that happened. He blindly walked into an apartment full of cops, that turned around and perp walked him back out to a street full of reporters. I guess he thought all those cop cars and news vans around the building were for someone else. Don't get it wrong though. He wasn't totally innocent. He must have had a reason for having all those guns, but I'm not talking about that. I'm talking about the lady up in apt. 5D, that he was cheating on my mom with. Some how she found out about it, and I guess this was payback. Sorry Manuel.

I got off the hook with just a minor suspension from school; and I had to see a counselor once a week. Manuel got 7 years. Better him than me.

Soon after, mom and I left the Bronx and moved to Queens. For some odd reason she wanted to stay in New York. We ended up moving to a part of Queens called Far Rockaway, with some big, fat, sloppy dude that she recently met. Where does she find these motherfuckers? I don't know, but right off the bat we had tension. He didn't like me and I didn't like him. And I let it be known. I'd curse that fat bastard out every time I got the chance, in front of any and everybody. I know my mom was embarrassed, and she did try disciplining me. Unfortunately time out didn't work. Grounding me didn't work. Taking away my toys didn't work either. What I needed was an old fashioned ass whipping, but that wasn't going to happen. Her new boyfriend, Milford, (what kind of fucked up name is that?) really wanted to put hands on me. God bless her, because she would always say to him,

"ain't nobody gonna touch my baby but me."

I was never left alone in his company. I

guess Charlene didn't trust him.

Whenever we sat at the table to eat; I would take a few bites, then open my mouth so he could see all the chewed up food. That would get him heated. He would say,

"Close your fucking mouth while you're eating."~

I'd respond back with, "Don't tell me what to do, you ain't my daddy."

"All right you little bastard, you keep talking shit I'm gonna put my foot in your ass"

"No you won't. You're just mad that you're fat."

Then I'd look over to my mom for reassurance and she'd tell us both to cut it out.

"Can we for once have a nice quiet meal together?"

"Charlene you need to check your son, before I check him for you," Milford replied.

That's how the big arguments would start. They would argue all night behind that. I'd pray that one day she'd leave him. I just hated looking at him. I hated his heavy breathing and loud snoring when he would fall asleep on the couch. I hated him stinking up the bathroom, and always being wet with sweat. What did my mom see in him? How could she stay with a slob like that? I don't know why but she did. She stayed with him for a number of years. A little over seven to be exact, and that's when everything changed. I was on the heels of turning 14, coming into my own, and about to cause all kinds of havoc.

2 "AS FAR BACK AS I CAN REMEMBER, I ALWAYS WANTED TO BE A GANGSTER." - NICHOLAS PILEGGI

The long hot summer of 1999 was coming to an end, and I was preparing to start my first year of high school. Despite all the trouble that I got into in my preadolescent years, I still remained a fairly good student throughout grade school. It was my mom's constant break ups and make ups that disrupted our home the most. We would find ourselves temporarily living in hotels, at friend's houses, and even in the car, whenever she and Milford got into it. A couple of days would pass, they'd make up, and we'd return home again like nothing ever happened. This scenario would repeat itself every couple of months; and each and every time, we would be the ones that would have to leave. Milford's fat ass never left, I'd ask my mom why, and she'd never have an answer.

All that back and forth shit was nerve racking and embarrassing, but it made me tough. It also caused me to get into a lot of fights. The teasing was never ending. I had to kick a couple of the more popular kids asses to make it stop, and that helped build my 'tough guy' reputation. It wasn't long before I was feared throughout the neighborhood.

That same energy continued well on into high school, and I leveraged it into a business; the business of extortion.

On the first day of school I started hemming kids up in the bathroom, and taking their lunch money. If they didn't have any money, they had to give up something to keep me off their ass. I got treated to video games, sneakers, and jewelry; just about anything I wanted I got from my fellow classmates. The generosity was overwhelming.

There was another shady kid around the school that everyone was kinda leery of also. He was a real funny looking cat, built on the skinny side, and always wore a little black beanie in the center of his head. Later on I found out it had something to do with his religion; he was Jewish.

His name was Sammy Singer. On the low, everyone called him "taps", because of the metal taps he wore on the bottom of all of his shoes, including his sneakers. One day he got in a fight with another student and he took off his shoe, hit the kid in the face and broke his nose. That shit was funny as hell.

I know he was supposed to be Jewish, but he looked more like the Arabs that worked in the bodegas around my way. He had olive colored skin and jet black curly hair. Anyway, we were in some of the same classes together, and every single time the class had to pair up for a project, he'd wind up being my partner. Barely a word would be exchanged between us, but we would always bust out the work, and get the best grade on that assignment.

One day when I was running the pockets of one of my generous classmates, a school security guard saw me take some cash from the kid, and decided to stick his nose in my very profitable business. He hollered,

"Hey… hey, what are you doing over there?"

I acted like I didn't hear him and started

to walk away. The guard kept on yelling,

"Young man, Young man, you hear me talking to you! Don't walk away!"

I slowly kept walking and made my way to the end of the hallway. I knew he was following close behind, but I ignored him. When I got to the end of the hall, I made a left turn and hauled ass. The chase was on!

"Stop!" he yelled.

I ran full speed down the steps, exited through the door and outside onto the street. I looked back, and this dude was still coming. He had a walkie talkie in his hand, and I could faintly hear him calling for back up. I took off running again. I ran up the street and headed towards a McDonalds restaurant, that all the kids hung out at when they cut class. It's next to the entrance of the Cross bay bridge. That bridge led to an all white town called Broad Channel, which was next to another all white town called Howard Beach. During that era, every nigga I knew, knew not to get caught in either of those towns; especially after dark.

I could have ran over the bridge and most likely got away, but I thought about the Memorial day parade that they had there last year; where some of New York's finest and bravest, aka police officers and firemen, dressed up in "black-face", and reenacted the scene of a black dude being dragged by a truck. So going that direction would have been a bad move.

Anyway, I figured that I could lose the security guards in the crowd at McDonalds; by now I had four of them after me. I dipped into the restaurant and tried to slide into the men's bathroom, but the door was locked.

"Shit!"

I then tried the women's bathroom, and that was also occupied.

Sitting in one of the booths watching the whole scene play out was none other than Sammy Singer, aka Taps. We made eye contact. He quickly got up out of his seat and started walking towards me. I was thinking to myself, I know this cat ain't gonna try and be a hero. You know how some white folks are, they just love putting their nose into other people's business. So I clinched my fist and was all set up to give him the knockout punch, when he said,

"Come on follow me."

I hesitated at first, then said fuck it, and

followed right behind him. We exited the side door facing the parking lot, weaved around a couple of cars and ended up by an old, rust colored Jaguar that he happened to have the keys to. We jumped in; he started it up, and pulled off. I slid down low in the passenger seat as we passed by the security detail, which now grew to about eight.

I mumbled to myself, "suckers!"

Then reached over and gave Taps a pound.

"Yo, I owe you one B."

"You don't owe me anything, but if you ever want to leave that petty shit alone and make some real dough, let me know," he replied.

I sarcastically responded,

"Real dough? You wanna school me on how to make some real dough? Nigga please. What you need to do is school me on how you gonna get some paint on this motherfucking car."

Trying to sound convincing he said,

"This is my grandfather's car. I just borrowed it. When I'm old enough to get my license I won't be driving a piece of shit like this, I'm gonna get a Porsche."

Chuckling, I looked at him and asked,

"You don't have a license?"

He quickly replied,

"I'm only 14, how old do you think I am?"

"I don't know. You damn near got a full mustache and beard. I thought you were like 19 or 20."

"Come on, a 20 year old in the ninth grade?"

Scratching my head I responded,

"Well uhh… maybe you got left back a few times."

We both burst out laughing.

After riding around a bit, I asked him to drop me off at Beach 86th St near the Hammel Houses housing projects.

Stretching as I got out the car I said,

"I had enough excitement for today. I'm about to get with this chick... We'll talk later, a'ight."

"Are you coming to school tomorrow?"

"Yeah, I'm not worrying about the security guards recognizing me; they think all black people look alike any way."

Looking confused he said,

"I thought you were Mexican."

"Oh you trying to be funny motherfucker?"

I slapped my hand on the roof of the car as he drove off. He was laughing hysterically; I don't know if it was because of the joke, or if he was laughing about the cloud of blue smoke that he left behind. After I finished coughing from all that pollution, I looked up at the tall building and proceeded to go in.

The chick that I stopped by the projects to see was my momma's good friend Tiffany. I've been banging her out for a couple of month's now. She used to babysit me when I was younger, but now we took our relationship to a whole different level.

She was a short chunky chick who sported a blond wig. Her hair matched her light brown complexion flawlessly, and along with her bubbly personality, she was real cool to be around. Looking back, I realize that she was one of those older women that been dogged out by men so much; she actually gave up on them. She thought that the love she found with a woman would feel the same and would satisfy her needs… She was wrong.

Her live in girlfriend, Kelly, thinks that I'm just Tiffany's Godson, and a playmate for her 12 year old daughter Keke. There was no reason for her to be suspicious. She had no clue at all that we were fucking. We often times got busy when she was right there in the house.

Tiffany would play it off and say,

"Robert your hair looks terrible. Come on, let me wash it and braid it back up for you."

We'd go into the bathroom turn the water on in the sink and get to screwing. She would always feel guilty afterward and say to me,

"This is wrong. This is really wrong. We need to stop this."

But the following week we'd be back at it again.

Getting back to Kelly, she was a real bull dagger. She was overly aggressive and acted manly; and I'll admit I was kinda scared of her. There was something sexy about her though. She would always walk around the apartment with a wife beater on, with no bra. Her titties sagged, but the highlight of it was seeing her nipples protrude through the shirt. She rocked a Mohawk haircut, had flowers tatted on her shoulder, and sported a nose ring. I'm not ashamed to say that she made my dick hard, and I think Tiff could sense the attraction. She would catch an attitude or find some reason to start an argument. A couple of times she caught me staring at her, and came up with the excuse that it was getting late, and that I should start to head home. Once, she went as far as to call my momma and tell her that I'd been hanging out at her house all day, just lying around eating up all of her food and shit, and for her to come get me.

Every time I remind her of that incident, she'd try and laugh it off and say that she was only playing; but I knew she wasn't, her ass was simply jealous.

One minute she wants to treat me like a grown man and wants me to do grown man things, the next minute she's quick to remind me that I'm a 14 year old, when I do something that she doesn't like.

And today was one of those days. She caught me staring at Kelly's ass again, and the look she gave me told me it was time to go... So I left.

I whistled my way down the hall to the elevator, and pushed the button. Then I waited, and waited, and waited.

"Don't tell me this shit is out of order again. I just came up on this thing."

These project elevators are always

breaking down. Since I was only on the fourth floor I decided to take the stairs. I walked into the stairwell and started making my way down the steps. All of a sudden the lights went out. It didn't faze me; the lights always flickered off and on in this building, it was normal. It was when I got to the second floor landing that things got weird. I heard a door slam, and then a bunch of footsteps running up in my direction. It wasn't totally dark in the stairway, a little bit of light crept in from the hallway at each landing. Unfortunately though, it wasn't enough to see the crew of guys who rushed me, knocked me down, and stomped me out.

Believe me, I tried to fight back. I grabbed a hold of one of the guy's legs who was doing the stomping, and pulled him down. He fell on top of me, and started punching me in the face. I covered my head with my arms to block a lot of the blows. Doing that made it easier for them to flip my pants pockets inside out, and take my money. They also snatched the little gold chain that I wore around my neck. Everything happened so fast I didn't realize the extent of my injuries. They left me curled up on the floor battered and bruised.

I eventually propped myself up against the wall, and began to wipe my face off with the bottom of my shirt. I tasted blood in my mouth, but I wasn't quite sure where it was coming from. I decided to go back to Tiffany's apartment to let her know what happened and also to change my shirt.

I knocked on her door. She peeped through the peep hole, but I had my back turned so she couldn't see my face. She knew it was me though; and said,

"What do you want Robert, I thought you were going home."

I turned to face the door and said,

"I just need to change my..."

Her door swung open before I could finish my sentence.~

"Jesus Christ what happened to your face!" she screamed.

"These dudes just jumped me in the stairwell… do I look that bad?"

She dragged me into her apartment and shuffled me into the bathroom.

"Come on Tiffany I'm not in the mood to fuck right now." I whispered.

She propped me in front of the mirror and said,

"Look at your face!"

I had a big gash from the top of the left side of my head, all the way down to my chin. You could see the white meat. I started feeling woozy and passed out.

I can't even remember how I got to the hospital, all I know is when I came to, I had a big bandage wrapped around my head, and the whole left side of my face felt real tight. Those cats fucked me up. My momma told me that I got 128 stitches in my face, 25 stitches on the top of my head, and another 10 behind my right ear.

Milford brought her to the hospital after she received the call from Tiffany. He was standing off to the side with a smirk on his face looking like he was glad it happened. I found out that Tiffany and Kelly carried me out the apartment and drove me to the hospital, while Tiffany's daughter Keke held a towel to my face to help stop the bleeding.

My momma kept on questioning Tiffany about the incident.

"What was he doing over your house anyway Tiff?"

"You know he always stops by and hangs out with us Charlene, this ain't nothing new."

"Why didn't you give him a ride home? You normally give him a ride home."

"I don't always give him a ride home Charlene you know that. I'm not to blame for this. I didn't have anything to do with this."

"I'm not blaming you, but then again I think you're partly responsible. You know where you live is fucked up. You should have been looking out for my son."

Raising her voice Tiffany replied,

"Like where you live is a whole lot better. It's fucked up over there too; just because you live in a house, that you don't own, you rent, you think it's so much better? Your next door neighbor sells crack out his basement."

"Lower your tone bitch, lower your tone."

"So now I'm a bitch Charlene? I didn't call you out your name."

"Yes bitch, yeesss! You wanna put my business all out in the street. You're lucky I only called you a bitch, and didn't smack that tacky-ass wig off your head."

"Wow Charlene, wow, it's like that?"

Kelly jumped in to try and calm the situation.

"Ladies, ladies, y'all need to chill."

Then Milford added his two cents.

"Yeah, y'all need to chill out with all that. This is embarrassing. All this arguing up here in the hospital, this discussion can wait."

"There's nothing to discuss," Charlene said, "Robert is just gonna stay his ass from over there."

For some reason Tiffany decided to make an emotional plea.

"Charlene, Robert can still come over. I'll pick him up if I have to. It doesn't have to be like that."

Kelly butted in and said,

"Tiffany it's not that serious. If Charlene doesn't want him to come over any more that's fine. We gotta respect that."

"Robert is like a son to me, and like a big brother to Keke. I have no problem picking him up or dropping him off if he wants to come by. I'll make sure that nothing happens to him again. I promise you that Charlene."

"Whatever bitch, whatever."

I was thinking to myself that Tiffany is gonna blow up our spot. She got everyone looking at her, like, why is she so adamant about me coming to her house? It was starting to look fishy.

Normally I would have said something to try and smooth this whole thing out, but the pain medication these doctors gave me, got a nigga nodding. So much so I could barely walk to Milford's car. But my momma was there to coddle me all the way.

She opened the rear door of the car and we both got in the back. Milford was sitting up front by himself. Before he pulled off he glanced up and looked through his rear view mirror at us and said,

"Am I you guy's chauffeur now?"

"Please don't start Milford, we just wanna go home," my mom said.

He shook his head and started to drive. During the ride my mom held my hand and caressed my head. Milford kept sucking his teeth and taking deep breaths. I don't know what was aggravating him so much, but something was bothering him. Bothering him so bad that he turned around and said,

"See Charlene that's the problem right there. You baby him to much. He doesn't need you to hold his hand. He be out here running in these streets thinking he's tough, he should expect things like this to happen. Karma just caught up with him."

"Milford, didn't I say that I didn't wanna talk about this right now? What's your problem?"

"That nigga right there is the problem," he replied, as his eyes zoomed in on me through the rear view mirror.

"You act like you're jealous of my son Milford. Are you jealous?"

That's when I interjected;

"Yeah Milford, are you jealous of me fat boy?"

He quickly swerved over to the side of the road and yelled,

"That's it, that's it!" He then threw the car into park and got out.

He stormed around to the back of the vehicle and opened the door, grabbed me by my shirt, and pulled me out.

"You're ass is walking home!"

My mom jumped out and ran around the back of the car to the side where we were, and pushed Milford.

"Are you crazy? Don't you put your hands on my son!" she yelled.

At first I thought he was gonna turn away like he normally does, but this time was different. He reacted. He pushed my mom back real hard. So hard that she flew off her feet and landed on her ass. I tried to jump in, but the meds had me moving so slow that Milford was able to catch me with an overhand right, straight to my forehead. He hit me so hard I saw a flash of light and immediately dropped to the ground.

My mom sprang back up to her feet and started swinging wildly at him. That's when I heard it, Crack!!! He slapped her in her face and knocked her out cold. As I struggled to get up and regain my balance, I watched him reach in the car, grab my mom's purse, and dump the contents and the purse onto her head. Then he calmly turned around, got back into his car and drove off.

"Ma... ma," I called out as I shook her head side to side in an attempt to try and make her regain consciousness. Her face was starting to swell and a large welt was becoming visible. When she came to, she stared at me for a few seconds and began to cry. My mom rarely ever shed a tear over anything; and especially not over some random ass nigga. Seeing that, hurt me more than getting jumped in the projects or Milford's punch to my head. Right then and there I made up my mind that he was gonna pay dearly for this.

As my mom and I slowly walked arm in arm to the nearest train station, I told her to call Tiffany. Despite their recent blow up, she'll always come through. You can count on her. But my mom was too embarrassed. She'd rather go get a hotel and spend the night there until she could figure out what to do next. Just as we were about to climb the stairs to the elevated train station I hear someone yell out "Charlene, Charlene, wait, wait!" Yelling through his car window it was that fat bastard Milford. He had circled back around looking for us, or rather her. "I'm sorry baby, I'm so, so, sorry. I didn't mean for that to happen. I lost control," he bellowed as he pulled up, and got out his car. "Can we just talk for a minute?" I can't believe my mom actually stopped to listen to this guy, after what just happened. "Back up" I yelled, as I tugged on my mom's arm in an attempt to pull her up the stairs.

"This is between me and your mother," he said. "Charlene, please just give me one minute, let me explain."

"There ain't nothing to explain," I said as I proceeded to move towards him. "Put your hands up and let's shoot this fair one."

I wasn't really ready for that, but I figured my bluff would work and make my mom listen to me rather than him. But she didn't. Instead she put her hand on my chest, pushed me back and said, "Just give us a minute."

I stood at the foot of the steps and waited, as my mom walked over to Milford's car and they commenced to talk. I couldn't hear but it looked like he was doing most, if not all of the talking. He was being all extra with his hand gestures, and pacing back and forth. I hoped my mom wasn't gonna fall for his bullshit. I could only imagine running over there and bashing him in his head, but due to my diminished physical condition, it wasn't the best time to do it. Plus this dude is huge. I would have needed a weapon of some sort. Usually there's garbage or some construction debris around the station that I could use as a weapon, but today it was spotless. I had to chill. Only thing I could do was ice grill him.

They were over there talking for a good 20 minutes when my mom began to flag me over.

"What?" I yelled.

"Come over here he wants to talk to you."

"I don't have nothing to say to that nigga."

"Come on Robert, let's squash this for now and go home. We can work it out later."

"What do you mean work it out later? ... There ain't nothing to work out. And I know you're not going home with this nigga after what he just done to you," I replied.

Hesitantly she responded with, "What you want me to do Robert?… huh? What you want me to do? He apologized."

"Well I'll see you later then."

I turned and began to jog up the stairs to the train.

My mom started screaming, "Wait a minute Robert, wait!"

I ignored her and continued to run up the stairs and on to the station platform. I looked back down from where I was standing, and watched as Milford stopped my mom from running up after me. They exchanged a few words, then got in the car together and slowly pulled away. I guess they figured I would go back to Tiffany's, or make my way home later, but I didn't. I ended up spending not only this night, but many nights under the boardwalk at

Rockaway beach. I didn't think I'd be safe staying in the projects with Tiffany, because as of right now I don't know who rolled on me or why I was rolled on. For all I know it could've just been random. And I definitely wasn't about to go home as long as Milford was living there.

3 "THERE ARE PLACES ON A MAN'S HEAD THAT ARE AS HARD AS A ROCK. YOUR HEAD'S ACTUALLY STRONGER THAN YOUR BODY. AND YOU DON'T HAVE TOO MANY INSTRUMENTS UP THERE WORKIN'." - JOE FRAZIER

It had been a couple of weeks since I last saw or had any contact with my mom. After everything that happened, I still hoped that she was doing okay. Despite all the worrying I did, it didn't change how I felt. I was still upset with her for leaving with that faggot Milford.

If I didn't know any better, I'd swear he had her brainwashed or something. In the past, if any of her boyfriends would have even thought about doing her wrong, she'd be out, and there would be no coming back. Now she acts like she can't live without this nigga. All he had to do was sweet talk her a little bit and she'd instantly forgive him.

I was done with that bullshit; I had to find my own way out here on these streets, and it was a lot tougher than I thought. Besides having no where really to stay, I was also low on money, and this situation had to be resolved fast. Winter was on its way, and it gets deathly cold out here in the Rockaways; especially by the beach. The little chump change I made during the day panhandling, and the stick-ups I did at night on the boardwalk, kept me afloat for a while, but I knew I couldn't do it all winter. Plus there was no way that I could continue to do robberies with bandages all over my face. It made it way too easy to be identified. I had to figure out a better plan.

The first step was to remove the stitches, which I did. I picked them out of my face one stitch at a time, but the results weren't that great. The scar it left looked way worse than the bandage, and now at this stage in the game, I had no choice but to live with it.

On to the next step. The mission was to try and catch up with Taps. I had to find out if he really had a way to make some quick money like he claimed. He told me to holla at him when I was ready, but I didn't know where he lived and didn't have his number. So I headed to the only place where I knew I could find him, and that was school.

He wasn't a regular class cutter like I was. In order to catch up with him, I would actually have to come to class. As much as I hated to, I did, that's how desperate I was.

Being absent for so long I didn't know what they were studying; what assignments were due or nothing. I didn't even have a notebook.

When I walked into home room the teacher did a double take before asking me if I was a student there.

Without hesitation I quickly answered,

"Yes ma'am. You don't remember me? My name is Robert Riley. I've been absent for a while because I had an accident."

I pointed to my face.

She stared at me for a solid minute then said,

"Oh, ok, sorry to hear that Robert. Do you have a doctors note?"

Earlier that morning, I had finessed a classmate into writing a note for me on the computer in the school library. I figured that the teacher would ask for one, and I was right.

I reached in my pocket, pulled out the note, and placed it on her desk.

"Okay, take a seat, and we'll see if we can catch you up to speed afterwards."

She didn't take her eyes off of me for the entire time I spent trying to find an empty chair.

If it was my scar that was bothering her, I wished she would've said something instead of looking at me all crazy. At least the kids in the class who I caught staring, had the decency to turn away whenever I looked back at them. This lady wouldn't even blink. She was all up in my grill.

Thank God that the tap dance kid himself, Sammy Singer aka Taps, entered the classroom. He temporarily took the shine off me with all the noise he made. The tick tacking sound that emanated from his shoes, echoed through the room with every step he took.

He spotted me sitting in the back of the classroom, and nonchalantly walked up to my desk and said,

"Where you been hiding? Were you scared to come to school? Bro, nothing would have happened to you, I would've had your back."

I tried to play stupid. "Yo B, what are you talking about?"

"I heard you got rolled on in the Hammel houses. Some kid was saying that you got duffed out… Damn, did they do that to your face?"

He was talking so loud that I started looking around the room to see who all was listening. After he realized what he was doing, he quickly lowered his voice almost to a whisper. And It was a good thing he did; I was starting to get heated.

"Yo, you remember that kid that you told me you robbed that day, just before I saw you at McDonalds?" he asked.

"Yeah I remember, and?..."

"Well he lives in that building, and I over heard him talking about it in the lunch room a couple of weeks ago. He said that his cousin, along with two other dudes, jumped you."

"Oh, so you think he had something to do with setting me up?"

"I don't know. All I can say is that he was laughing and joking about it."

I nodded my head and tried to pretend like it didn't bother me, but it did."

"A'ight, I got something for those niggas. Just watch."

In reality I didn't, but I had to save face. In fact, I didn't want to have nothing to do with those cats at all. I was willing to lick my wounds and keep it moving.

I honestly didn't expect this funny looking Jewish kid from Belle Harbor to pull my card like that, and I definitely didn't expect him to know everything that was going on in my hood. But he was like a magnet to it. He knew the slang, he knew a lot of the people, and he even tried to look the part. Mind you, he looked crazy out of place doing it, but he still tried.

I couldn't put my finger on it, but something just wasn't quite right with him. At the time I didn't care, all I was interested in was making money. That was the only thing on my mind, and I explained that to him without going into great detail.

"Yo homey I'm going through some things right now, and I need to make some money," I said.

Before he could reply the teacher rudely interrupted.

"Excuse me gentlemen, is there something you would like to discuss with the class?"

We both shook our heads no.

"Well would you kindly join us and open your text book to page 45? You two will have to share since Robert doesn't have a book. Thank you."

We promptly ended our conversation and joined in with the class.

The teacher still couldn't stop looking at me. Every time I looked up at the blackboard, she would be staring dead in my face. It was like she was trying to confirm to herself that I was who I said I was. I know it sounds crazy, but that's how it felt.

Taps and I had to wait till the class was over to continue our discussion, and it seemed like it dragged on forever. Once it was over we had to talk quick. He didn't want to be late for his next class.

"Yo B, hook me up. I need to make some money," I said.

"Oh I thought you said it was bullshit," he replied.

"I don't remember saying that, but if I did, my bad. So what's the deal? You gonna put me on or what?"

Looking excited he said, "Meet me out by my car after school. If you wanna make some money today, BE ON TIME!"

"Okay calm down, I'll be there… So, let me get this straight; now it's your car and not your Grandpa's?"

"Why are you being an asshole?"

"Yo B what's the problem? I just asked a simple question; why do you get so uptight every time I say something about your car?"

"I'm not uptight. You're trying to be funny, but you're not. You're corny… Just don't be late."

He stormed off to his class.

By the end of the day, as promised, I was there waiting patiently by his car. He was so adamant about me being on time, and he was no where in sight. So I sat on the hood and waited.

While sitting, I noticed a black Ford Crown Victoria, with tinted windows, slowly circling the parking lot. At first I didn't pay it no mind, but something in my gut told me to keep an eye on it. I followed it around and watched it as it moved closer to where I was. Once it hit the aisle where Tap's car was parked, I decided that it was time to break out. Suddenly the car sped up and stopped right in front of me. Two guys hopped out the vehicle and repeatedly yelled,

"Get on the ground! Get on the ground!"

They had their guns drawn and the whole nine.

At first I was gonna comply. I squatted like I was about to get down, but changed my mind midway, and took off running. They were gonna have to work for their pay that day.

I ran right into the busy street in front of the school. A couple of cars blew their horns and skidded to a stop while I scooted past them. I dodged and weaved my way through the rest of the traffic until I made it to the other side of the street; then sprinted full speed toward the train station.

I ran as fast as I could, but unfortunately I couldn't out run their radio. I made it about three blocks before I was cut off and surrounded.

They roughed me up, slapped on the cuffs, and threw me in the back of a squad car.

The next thing I knew I was sitting in the interrogation room at the 100th precinct.

One of the officers handcuffed me to a long bar, that was mounted on a wall, and then left the room. Shortly there after two detectives walked in. One of them took a seat directly across from me, and his partner sat a little further back by the door. The one sitting across from me said,

"Do you know why you're here?"

"No I don't," I replied.

"What happened to your face?"

"I had an accident."

"What kind of accident? A slip and fall, a car accident, what?"

"What does my face have to do with me being here? When can I go?"

The detective reached into his pants pocket, pulled out a ring of keys, leaned over and un-cuffed me.

"Do you want something to drink? A soda or something?"

"No sir I don't want a soda. Am I free to go?"

He looked back at his partner and said,

"Get him a soda. Do you like coke?"

Before I could answer he said,

"Get him a coke, we're gonna be here for a while."

I'm looking at this guy like where is he going with this?

Then he begins to ask a bunch of stupid ass questions like; what grade I'm in, do I have a girlfriend, and do I play any sports?

This type of questioning went on for like three and a half hours, and I was starting to get tired. I folded my arms on the table in front of me, and laid my head down.

Bam!

He slapped the table hard with his hand and said, "Wake up, you can't sleep now, we're just getting started."

I told him that I was tired and didn't wanna talk anymore, but he wouldn't let up. Then the conversation started to go left.

"Ain't it wrong for you to question me without my momma or a lawyer being here? I'm only a minor. I think it's against the law and you can get in trouble for that."

That's when he flipped on me and began to yell.

"YOU'RE GONNA TELL ME WHAT THE FUCKING LAW IS? I'M THE FUCKING LAW, YOU HEAR ME! AND I'M GONNA LOCK YOUR LITTLE SPIC ASS UP!"

I was shocked on how quick he changed from being all cool calm and collected; to foaming at the mouth. He called me everything except a child of God. He even told me how he was gonna deport me back to Mexico; not knowing that I'm just a light skinned nigga from around the way. I wasn't really fazed by all the racial stuff he was saying. I found it funny. I even started laughing. That's when he got in my face and snatched me up by my collar.

"YOU THINK THIS IS FUNNY? I'LL SHOW YOU WHAT FUNNY IS!"

His partner, who'd been sitting quietly the whole time, jumped out his seat and pulled him off me.

"Take a break, let me talk to him," he said.

He then escorted his frustrated partner out of the room, and quickly came back in. He shut the door and removed his suit jacket, slid a chair directly in front of me and sat down. He stared at me for a moment, then took a deep breath before he started talking.

"You know, you're being accused of some pretty serious crimes. Sexual battery in the course of an armed robbery is not a joke my friend."

I couldn't believe what this guy was saying. I thought I heard him wrong.

"What?! What did you say? Sexual what? I didn't sexually do nothing to nobody!"

"Well you've been identified. The woman

pointed you out my man. But what I'm trying to understand is why would you go back and flaunt it in her face?"

"What are you talking about?" I replied.

"You kids now a days are something else. You got the nerve to come into her classroom, and act like nothing happened."

"Her classroom? I haven't been to school in almost a month!"

"It didn't happen at school pal. It happened at the beach, on the boardwalk, a few weeks ago. Does that refresh your memory?"

"On the boardwalk?"

My mind started racing. I tried to remember all the people I robbed in the past few weeks. I was willing to admit to a robbery, but not that sexual shit, and I told him that. I also told him that I didn't remember seeing any of my teachers out there, but he wasn't trying to hear it.

"Buddy let me put it to you like this. She said her and her husband were jogging on the boardwalk one evening, when a kid, that fits your description perfectly, came up to them from out of nowhere. At gunpoint, you demanded that they give you all of their money. She said her husband didn't have nothing on him, but she gave up the 20 bucks she had tucked away in her bra. According to her, after she gave up the money, you fondled her breasts and squeezed her ass before you ran off."

"That bitch is lying!... I remember robbing a couple. It was kinda dark so I didn't get a good look at their faces. But I remember the lady taking the money out of her sock, not her bra, and throwing it on the ground. I never touched that bitch! I swear to God!"

"So you're admitting to the armed robbery?"

"I didn't have a gun; I had my two fingers pointed under my shirt to make it look like I had one."

"Okay, what I need you to do is write your statement down on this paper, sign it, and we'll go from there. You did some bad things, but it's good that you manned up and took responsibility for it. Now you can clear your conscience."

After I signed the statement, I realized that I fucked up. I should've stood my ground, and kept my mouth shut until I had a lawyer present. But this was the first time I dealt with the police on my own. I always had my momma there to do all the talking, and fight all my battles.

My bond was set at $20,000. As much as I wanted to, I didn't call my ma. I didn't want her to have to ask Milford for anything, or be out in the streets scrambling trying to get me out. I had to try and handle this situation on my own.

4 "BUT I SAY TO YOU, LOVE YOUR ENEMIES AND PRAY FOR THOSE WHO PERSECUTE YOU, SO THAT YOU MAY BE SONS OF YOUR FATHER WHO IS IN HEAVEN; FOR HE MAKES HIS SUN RISE ON THE EVIL AND ON THE GOOD, AND SENDS RAIN ON THE JUST AND ON THE UNJUST." - JESUS CHRIST

The things that I experienced during my first couple of days inside, were unlike anything I'd ever experienced before. Mind you, this was jail, not prison; and if I already had issues in there, I could only imagine what prison was gonna be like.

All of that keeping it real and trying to be hard shit, went right out the window as soon as I arrived. I was surrounded by guys just as tough or even tougher than I was, and had done things far more worse.

The conditions were so bad that I contemplated calling my mom to see if she could get me out; even when after I promised myself that I wouldn't.

Some of the fights I witnessed were brutal. Kids were getting stomped out left and right while the guards clearly looked the other way. Once in a while in their futile attempt to get the fighting to cease, one of them would yell "cut it out," but that did little to stop a motherfucker who was intent on putting in work.

They had so many of us packed in one big cell, that if anyone got seriously hurt, they could potentially be laid up in the corner for hours before any of the staff would know that they were injured.

Fights between inmates and guards didn't happen to often, but when it came to inmate against inmate; shit would kick off damn near every hour. You would instantly know when something popped off because of the rush of people running to one side of the cell. Guys would be climbing over and knocking each other down in order to get out of the way. With all of that commotion going on, it was hard to tell who was fighting who.

Everyone in there was cliqued up. I rarely saw a one on one fight. It didn't matter if you minded your own business or not, you were getting touched. I knew my time was coming.

I ended up having a few words with a couple of kids from Brooklyn who claimed that they were Blood. At the time I thought they were full of shit; that they were just wannabe gangsters who watched too many west coast rapper's videos. Who knew that there were actual Bloods and Crips in New York back then.

The tension wasn't initiated by me, they were the ones who started everything, with the whole thinking that I'm Mexican shit. They insisted that I move to the other side of the cell with the Hispanic dudes. It was like a flashback to Mrs. Ford's elementary school class. Only this time, to avoid any trouble, I decided to do what they asked.

But there was push-back. I wasn't welcomed by the Spanish dudes either. They knew right off the bat that I wasn't one of them without even hearing me speak.

I went back to the original spot where I was standing, and again, the so called

Bloods tried to force me to go to another area; the area near the toilet. They knew that it stunk over there but still pressed me to go; trying to be funny. I wasn't having it, and after a little back and forth with them, I wound up swinging on the main guy who was talking all the shit. I got him good too, but that was the only punch I got off. After that, just about everyone in the cell jumped me.

I don't know how long it took before the C.O.'s got there, but when they came, they pulled me out, took me to get patched up, and returned me to the very same cell that they took me out of..

Contemplating round two, I stood with my back planted against the wall to give myself a better view from all angles of the cell. I made up my mind that no one was gonna come up from behind and hit me in the back of the head like before. Just as I was positioning myself, an officer started calling out names.

"Ramirez, Reynolds, Riley (that's me), Rodriquez."

They took us out of the cell one by one, made us line up against the wall, and then chained us together. We were led out to a van, and taken to a different facility that they said was going to be less crowded.

We ended up in the Bronx at a jail called the Vernon C Bain center; nicknamed the 'Boat.'

It was some type of cargo ship, made into a jail, that never sailed out into the water. This thing stayed docked the entire time I was there.

The dude that I was cuffed to in the van, said that he'd been locked up at this facility before, and that it wasn't that bad. To me it was hell. It was dark, dingy, and cold inside. The only good part about being there was that I was finally going to be able to take a shower. Other than that, I had to make do with everything else whether I liked it or not.

It was noisy as hell in that place. It seemed like every sound was magnified ten times the level of what it normally should have been. It was becoming unbearable. I think it was causing everyone to be angry and short fused, including the correction officers. They were handing out beat downs on a regular basis over minor shit.

If I wasn't battling with them, I was battling depression.

My trial kept getting postponed, and I had three different court appointed lawyers in less than a year. The future was looking bleak. So bleak that I started to cut myself. I know it sounds crazy but it made me feel better. It was sort of a stress reliever. However, there was one time that I cut myself a little bit too deep.

I never saw blood squirt out my wrist like that before. In less than a minute the entire front of my jumpsuit was completely covered in blood; but I didn't panic, I simply sat there on the side of my bunk and stared into space. Lucky for me a C.O. was making her rounds and happened to see the bloody mess. It was her very first day on the job, and I was surprised that she remained so calm. She quickly brought in the troops and they whisked me out of the cell and took me down to medical. That's when the new C.O. and I realized that we knew each other. This new officer was none other than Tiffany's girlfriend, Kelly.

"Oh my God! Robert? Is that you? What are you doing in here? What happened to you?" she asked.

All her fellow co-workers were looking at her like; where do you know this kid from?

She explained it to them before anyone opened their mouths to ask.

"He's a friend of mines, son. I knew him ever since he was a little boy."

She continued to fill them in with all the details as they wheeled me down to medical.

After I was treated, I was relocated to a different cell. I was moved from my previous location, to an area where they kept all the nut jobs. Kelly didn't work in that section, so I didn't see her for a while after that. I eventually ran into her again one day on my way to court, and we had a brief exchange. She was walking by the holding cell that I was in, and I blurted out her name,

"Kelly!"

She stopped, backed up, and peaked In.

"Hey Robert, how are you making out? Everything okay?"

Before I could answer she continued rambling.

"I want you to know that I told Tiffany that you were here and we contacted your mom. I checked around and found out that you haven't had any visitors, so I figured she didn't know. Why didn't you contact her?"

"It's a long story," I replied.

"Robert come on, you're in here hurting yourself, getting into fights with the inmates and officers, what's going on with you? I saw your paper work and you got some serious charges pending. Please tell me you didn't do all the things they said you did."

"I didn't, that's all I can say right now. I didn't."

Looking like she didn't believe me she said, "Okay Robert, I'll try and do what I can, but, I'm on probation, and I want to keep my job. Understand?"

She gave me a long serious stare as if she was saying, "Don't fuck up my shit," before she walked off.

I knew that it wouldn't be long before I saw and heard my mom's voice again. I only wished it could had been postponed a little while longer. Jail had broken me, and I didn't want her to see me in the state that I was in. They had me on meds and everybody in there thought that I was 7:30. I had to see a quack once a week and I was being constantly monitored. I not only felt bad, I looked bad.

The very next day, I didn't get one visit, I got two. The woman beat my momma here.

I'm talking about Good old Tiffany. She broke down into tears as soon as I entered the visitors room. I was already embarrassed for what I had done to myself, now I had this woman in there hooping and hollering in front of all the inmates. I started to turn around and go back to my cell. Even the guards had to tell her to chill out and calm down.

I was like, "Damn Tiff I ain't dead! Why you in here falling out like it's my funeral or something."

After she finally pulled herself together, she began to hit me with nonstop questions. Who? What? Where? When? Why? And how? She ran her mouth so much I stopped paying attention. All I heard was waa waa waa, on some straight Charlie Brown shit. Her excessive talking made the time fly by quick. The only thing I could remember her saying before she left was, "We gonna get you out."

I didn't know who, 'we' was, but I hoped that they could make it happen.

Next up was my mom Charlene. It was tough seeing her. I was trying to hold back the tears as much as she was. I haven't seen or had any contact with her in close to a year, and I didn't like what I saw. She lost a crazy amount of weight, had on a dingy jacket, and some type of scarf was wrapped around her head. Her nails were all broken and chipped up with no polish, and she was wearing dark sunglasses. When she sat down in front of me she didn't take her glasses off, so I asked her to. I wanted to look her in her eyes. I hoped to God that she wasn't smoking! That's a sure fire way to find out if someone is; just look into their eyes. They could have been drug free for over ten years but a crack head's droopy eyes always gives them away. She removed the glasses and I was stunned. They weren't drooping, it was worse. She had two black eyes! Before she could ask what happened to me, I asked what happened to her. She started out by saying, "Things are not good Robert. It's not good at all."

The more she talked the more her eyes filled up with tears.

"Milford and I have been fighting. I've been trying to leave but I can't."

"What do you mean you can't," I replied.

"He won't let me. He'll show up to my job, he follows me around, and he threatens me."

"Why don't you call the cops on him?"

"I tried, but he always leaves right before they get there. And when he comes back he apologizes and tells me that it won't happen again, but it always does. I don't know what to do. I'm scared and I'm stressing out even more since I found out about you. I could just roll over and die… What happened to you baby? How'd you wind up in here? I thought you were staying with Tiffany."

"Why would you think that ma? I got jumped by people who live in her building. Why would I go back? But forget about me right now. We gotta figure out how to get you out your situation. I'm gonna kill that fat bastard when I get out of here!"

"Baby calm down let's take this one step at a time. First, I already have $500 of your bail money. I just need a little more time to get the rest."

Looking deflated I said, "$500? I guess I'll be sitting in here for another 10 years. My bail might as well be a million dollars."

"Why are you being so negative? I only need 10% of what their asking to get you out," she replied.

"10% of what? $20,000?

"Yes Robert 10% of $20,000 which is

$2,000, and I have $500 of that."

"So I've been sitting in here all this time when all I needed was $2,000?"

"Well no one knew where you were, and that's your own fault. I'll find a way to get the rest of the money and get you out of here as soon as possible. Just hang tight a little while longer."

"You don't have any friends that you could borrow the money from, and I'll pay them back when I get out?" I asked.

"How you gonna pay them back Robert? You ain't got no job. You don't even have your working papers boy. What are you gonna do rob people and get locked back up all over again? You're not thinking smart Robert. Besides, none of my friends have any money. The only one who probably has the money is Milford."

I quickly cut her off and said, "Don't ask that nigga for shit! I'd rather stay in here forever, that's my word!... What about Tiffany did you ask her?"

"Tiffany and Kelly gave me $200 of the money. You know they don't got it like that. Kelly just started her new job working in here, she just recently got her first paycheck. And Tiffany ain't making any money working at the dollar store; she can barely make ends meet. You're gonna have to cool out for a little bit and let momma work things out. Don't worry I'll get the money even if I have to start stripping part time to get it."

"Come on ma, really? Ain't nobody gonna pay to see some old lady take her clothes off."

"36 is not old! And besides I look damn good!"

I didn't wanna say it out loud, but my immediate thought was that during the course of one of their fights, Milford must had broken all the mirrors in the house. There was no other logical reason for my mom to come outside looking the way that she did. Lord knows I wanted to tell her that, but I didn't want to embarrass her; I loved her to much to hurt her feelings.

But before she left, I made sure to mention another possible way to get the rest of the money. I told her about Taps and the plan he offered me, but it fell on deaf ears. She was totally against going to see some random Jewish kid, that she didn't know, about money. She told me not to worry, that she'd figure it out on her own. All I could do was hope and pray that she would.

5 "YOU GOT NOTHING TO LOSE. YOU DON'T LOSE WHEN YOU LOSE FAKE FRIENDS." - JOAN JETT

My situation was starting to get a little bit better. I was getting visits once a week from both my Mom and Tiffany, and I had Kelly looking out for me in there as well. She would sneak in food, and magazines, and also pass along messages to other inmates that I was cool with. I had been there for about 14 months now, still with no trial date set, and no clue on when or if I'd ever get bonded out. My mom had been trying to raise the money for the past 3 months with no luck, all the while continuing to get her ass beat by Milford. I needed to get up out of there so I could deal with this guy. That was the main reason why on her visit this particular day, I insisted that she go and try to find Taps since her strategy to raise money wasn't working. I had to remind her that I'd been locked up since November of 98, and now it was January of 2000, and I wasn't trying to celebrate another birthday in there. Y2K came and went without a single computer glitch to help set me free, so this was my last resort.

I asked her, "Ma would it kill you to talk to Taps just to see what he had to say?"

After a little bit of heeing and hawing she eventually agreed.

I described him to her the best that I could. I gave her a description of the car he drove and everything. I told her that he shouldn't be hard to find. That he had a unique look; no one else at Beach Channel High school came even close to resembling him.

My description was dead on. The next day she was able to locate him within minutes of arriving at the school. She spotted him just as he was getting out of his car. Feeling a little apprehensive, she took caution in the way she approached him. The whole idea of meeting up with this kid was weird to her, and she was worried about what people would think if they saw her interacting with him. But she made a promise to me and she kept her word.

"Excuse me… umm is your name Sammy?" she asked.

Taps, looking a little unsure on how to answer said, "Uh, yes I am."

"Hi, I know you don't know me but I'm sure you know my son Robert. Robert Riley."

Feeling a little bit more at ease he replied, "Oh okay yes I know Robert."

"I'm his mom Charlene," she extended her arm out to shake his hand. "I really hate to bother you first thing in the morning, I know you're on your way to class, but he asked me to reach out to you about some work. Robert got himself in some trouble and he's now locked up. We've been trying to raise the money for his bail."

As she talked, Taps was studying her like a book. He was checking her out from head to toe, and wasn't at all discreet about it.

"I don't know if you can, or may know someone who can help us, but we would be real appreciative."

"How much do you need? How much is his bail?" Taps asked.

"I'm so embarrassed to be coming at you with this, but his bail is $2,000. I managed to raise 800 of it, so twelve is what we need."

"Well the job I had for Robert I don't think you'll want to do, but I can lend you the money and we can figure out how to pay me back later."

Charlene couldn't believe what she just heard and asked him to repeat what he said. Tap's again confirmed that he would lend her the money and she instantly replied, "God bless you young man! Thank you! Whatever we need to do to repay you we will.

"How soon do you need it?"

"Whenever you can get it to me will be fine. I'll give you my number and…"

He cut her off.

"I'll give it to you now, we just have to go to my house and get it." As he motioned to his car he said, "Hop in."

She hesitantly said, "I can wait till later… I don't want you to miss your class."

"There's nothing important going on right now, besides I don't live that far away so it won't take long."

It took a little convincing but she finally agreed to go with him to get the money. They jumped in his grandfather's car, and drove a few miles west into the Belle Harbor area of the Rockaways where he lived. They pulled up to a large brick three level home. Despite it being the winter and nothing was in bloom, the home showcased a manicured lawn and beautiful landscaping. A menorah was still sitting in the front picture window from the past Jewish holiday. Charlene was still feeling uneasy about this whole transaction. She looked at the gorgeous home and then at Taps and said, "I'll wait here in the car okay?"

"Don't be silly come on in it's gonna take a little while to count it up."

"What will your parents say? Won't they ask who I am, and why I'm with you?

"My parents are in Israel. Even If they were home, what are they going to say? It's none of their business. Stop worrying."

The first thing that popped into her head was; *if he was my child I would wanna know who he's bringing in and out of my house. These white folks raise their kids a lot different. They give their children way more leeway.*

After a little back and forth Taps persuaded her to come inside. Though thoroughly impressed, she didn't want him to notice how *'open'* she was by the decor and layout of the home. He gave her a brief tour, and then guided her upstairs into his room to get the money.

"Who's room is this? Your parents?" she asked.

"No this is my room."

"You have a bathroom with a Jacuzzi in your bedroom? Wow it must be nice," she said as she admired the fixtures.

Taps closed the bedroom door behind him, stepped into his walk in closet and grabbed a shoebox off a top shelf. He opened the box, took out a bundle of cash, strolled over to his dresser and started to count it. Charlene looked on in amazement. In the middle of him counting it out he looked over at Charlene and said, "I know how you can pay me back."

"Okay, how?"

"Take your clothes off."

"What?!"

"You heard me, take your clothes off," he demanded.

Charlene began to get a nervous feeling in her stomach.

"Boy are you crazy? This wasn't part of the deal. You can keep your fucking money I'm leaving," she said.

"You ain't going no where. You're going

to do exactly what I tell you to do. Now get naked!" he yelled, as he pulled out a revolver that he had hidden under his shirt.

"Why are you doing this? I thought you and my son were friends," she said as she unbuttoned her blouse.

With the gun pointed at her head he screamed, "Fuck your son! Hurry up and take your bra and your panties off, I don't have all day!"

Now completely nude, Charlene tried to cover up her body with her arms. "Put your fucking arms down!" he yelled, "Now turn around I want to see everything."

He stared intently as she turned full circle.

He then unzipped his pants and forced her to give him a blow job. Tears ran down her face as she performed the act.

"Now get up off your knees, turn around and bend over the bed!" he commanded. He penetrated her vaginally while he simultaneously stuck the barrel of the gun in her anus. She screamed out in pain. The louder she screamed the more violently he pushed the barrel of the gun inside her.

Although it only lasted a few minutes; for Charlene it seemed like it went on for hours. When it was finally over she didn't know what to do, what to think, or what to say. Taps collapsed in the bed alongside of her. She looked at him in disgust as he laid there with his Superman underoos wrapped around his ankles. He was still holding the gun in his hand and breathing heavily.

Charlene slowly got up, gathered her clothes, and started to get dressed.

When she was done she calmly asked, "Can I go?"

"Sure," he replied as he sniffed the barrel of his gun. "You need a ride?"

"No I'll walk."

she moved toward the bedroom door and began to open it.

"Ok, well aren't you gonna take the money?" he asked.

"No I don't want your money."

"Oh now you don't want my money? The reason why you came here in the first place was for the money, and now you don't want it? Remember you approached me I didn't come to you, so I don't know why you're all bent out of shape."

She looked back at him and said, "You fucking raped me motherfucker!"

"If you feel like you were raped, go to the police. In fact I'll take you. But please don't forget to tell them how you came to me; a 16 year old kid, for $1200. Tell them how you met me in my school parking lot, willingly got into my car, and came to my house while my parents were away. What does that sound like to you? Hmmm, sounds like a hooker to me. And a high priced one at that. What do you think?"

Standing in the doorway to his bedroom, she took a moment to take in all of what he said. The stack of money that was on his dresser was still there for the taking, and after mulling everything over in her head, she quickly grabbed it, stuffed it in her purse, and said,

"Drop me off at the train station."

He rolled off of the bed, pulled up his pants and they left.

6 "THERE IS ALWAYS SOME MADNESS IN LOVE. BUT THERE IS ALSO ALWAYS SOME REASON IN MADNESS." - FRIEDRICH NIETZSCHE

"I was free! Thank you Jesus, God the father, and the Holy Spirit!"

Even if it was only temporary. I knew that my case still had to be tried, but at that moment, I wasn't even trying to think about it.

I planned on enjoying every minute of my freedom. I had my dear momma Charlene to thank, and I can't forget about my main man Taps who came through with the bread.

Speaking of bread, I was feening to taste some real food again, and our first stop was the Dallas BBQ's restaurant on the West side of Manhattan. I remember ordering the sticky wings, and they were prepared just the way I liked; hot and sweet, with a couple of feathers still on them.

To be in the company of my momma, Tiffany, and Tiffany's daughter Keke, who by the way, in the last 15 or 16 months, had bloomed into a real dime piece; was a blessing. I tried my best not to stare at her, because her mom was quick to get jealous. If I had the opportunity to talk to Keke alone, I definitely would have pushed up. We were more age compatible, and had more things in common with each other, than I did with her mother. But celebrating my release, and enjoying a good meal, is what we were supposed to be doing. I didn't want to cause any drama.

Over dinner we discussed my living arrangements. My mom didn't want me to move back home right away, due to the problems that she was having with Milford. She was scared that we'd get into it, that I probably would do something to him, and be sent right back to jail. It was decided that I'd stay with Tiffany for the time being. Boy oh boy, she was excited about that. I guess she figured she'd get all the dick she wanted with me living there. Maybe a year ago I would have felt just as excited, but not anymore. I didn't know if something had changed in me, or if I came to the realization that it would be a fucked up thing to do to Kelly. Especially after she held me down for those few months. I felt kinda shaky about going back there period. Just thinking about stepping foot inside that building made me uneasy. Everything that happened to me there, was still fresh in my mind, and I really felt I had to be on my guard going back. My mom told me not to hang in the hallways or anywhere outside of the building. She basically wanted me to be a prisoner in Tiff's apartment. I had been locked up long enough. I wasn't gonna let anyone keep me from going outside or anywhere else I wanted to go. If anything, those cats who jumped me needed to be worried about me. I didn't express that to my mom over dinner, I only assured her that I'd be safe.

We switched the subject and tried to talk about something a bit lighter; that's when I brought up Taps and expressed how grateful I was to him for giving us the money for the bond. I was going on and on about how he was my main man, and how out of all the people we knew, it took someone that we really didn't know, to help us out. I jokingly explained how I was giving up Christianity and converting to Judaism; on some Sammy Davis Jr. shit. My mom got real quiet and kept looking down at her plate.

I continued on with the foolishness.

She eventually interrupted me, and with a touch of disdain in her voice said, "Can we please talk about something else?"

Tiffany took a break from gulping down her food and giggling, to mumble out, "What's wrong Charlene?"

"Nothing," she replied, as she tossed a couple of French fries around in her plate. "He's giving that boy way too much props. Just because he lent us some money doesn't mean he's your friend. All money ain't good money."

Refuting what she said I quickly responded,

"All money ain't good money? - Don't you see me sitting here ma? His money was good enough to bail me out so I'm okay with it. To me, it doesn't matter how he got it or what he had to do to get it. Come on, I know when you and Tiff were younger y'all probably did something strange for some change too."

Keke and I burst out laughing. Tiffany shook her head no and smiled. My mom on the other hand, started going off.

"What are you saying Robert? You think that I'd fuck some nigga for some money? You'd say that about your own mother? I'm tired of your shit you ungrateful spoiled rotten motherfucker!" she yelled.

Everybody's eyes in the restaurant zoomed in on our table.

"Ma, calm down I'm only joking. Why are you getting so upset? - And who said anything about you fucking some nigga?"

"Didn't you just say, do something strange for some change? What the fuck does that supposed to mean?" she asked.

"It could've meant anything. I wasn't thinking that. In fact you told me that if you had to you would strip to make some extra money. You said that, not me; remember that conversation? That's what I was referring to. Jesus Christ!"

She sat there silent for a few minutes, and then said, "Well you need to be careful how you say things, especially when it comes to me."

I always joked around with my mom and

said far worse things, but she never jumped down my throat like that before. I figured Milford had to have been stressing her out. That's the only thing I could think of. She's normally very upbeat, but from the moment I got out of jail she seemed to be down in the dumps.

After dinner we all hopped on the subway and headed back to the Rockaways. It was a long quiet ride, especially when no one was talking. Charlene's sudden outburst in the restaurant, had us all too nervous to say anything. So our conversation was at a minimum.

Her stop was first. She looked at me, gave me a hug, and told me she'd see me the next day, then she exited the train.

When Tiff, Keke and I reached our destination, we still had to walk about a block or two to reach the building. Every step I took I couldn't help but think about my mom, her situation, and all the bad things that I was planning on doing to Milford. I was so wrapped up in my thoughts that I didn't hear a word Tiffany or Keke were trying to say.

"Robert... Robert... do you hear me talking to you?" Tiffany asked.

"Sorry, my bad, I was daydreaming."

"What's going on with your mom?
… Lately it seems like she's stressing out even more than normal. I thought it was because of you, but you're home now and it seems like it's gotten even worse."

Keke chimed in and said, "I saw her in the supermarket last week. I spoke to her and she walked right passed me like she didn't even know who I was."

"Maybe she didn't," I said. "You've gotten so fine I wouldn't have known who you were either."

She started to blush.

"Stop playing Robert we're being serious," Tiffany said.

I wasn't about to tell them all my mom's business, or elaborate on any of the problems that she was having with Milford. If they wanted to know what was up with her, they needed to ask her. I continued to play the dummy role.

"Look, I really don't know what's going on with Charlene. Maybe it's that time of the month."

Tiffany sucked her teeth and said, "See Robert you're still playing. You don't take anything serious."

When we reached the building we took the stairs instead of the elevator, because they claimed it was acting up and getting stuck between the floors. Tiffany went on and on about how she didn't trust it, and tried to reassure me that if I took the stairs along with them, I wouldn't suffer the same fate as I did before.

"Robert, ain't nobody thinking about you. The shit that happened before was random. There's nobody staking out the stairway waiting for you. Me and Keke take the stairs everyday, you don't have to be scared."

"I ain't scared," I said. I just don't wanna be smelling like piss if they tackle me to the floor again. There's piss puddles all over the place. Besides, the only clothes I have is what I'm wearing on my back, Charlene is supposed to bring me some more of my stuff tomorrow. I just want y'all to know that I'll be sleeping in the buff on your couch tonight, so don't say I didn't warn you."

"Robert will you stop with your bullshit, I have something you can wear," Tiffany said. "You ain't laying your naked ass on my leather sofa."

Keke died laughing.

I was two seconds from asking Tiffany

what exactly did she mean by that, because I remember when both of our naked asses were rolling around on that very same sofa. But I wasn't gonna blow up her spot in front of her daughter.

We made our way down the piss smelling dimly lit hallway to the apartment. And we stood there for a good five minutes.

Tiffany had been living there now for almost as long as I've been alive, and she still had to fumble around with her keys in order to find the right one for the lock. She tried damn near every key on the ring, before the door suddenly flew open and Kelly greeted us.

"What up my peoples?!"

I was about to assume the position, because the first thing I saw was the uniform. She had just gotten home from work and hadn't yet changed out of her clothes.

"I couldn't wait any longer for you to open the Goddamn door Tiff, so I decided to give you a hand," Kelly said. "I was gonna sit here and wait to see how long it would take you to open the door, but I couldn't wait all night. You be killing me with that shit. Anyway, welcome home

Robert! - You know you gotta be on your best behavior, because I could lose my job behind you staying here, so we need to keep everything on the low, the same way we did on the boat. Cool?"

"Yo you got it Officer Kelly, but can I least come inside before you give me the run down?"

"Cut that officer shit out, and get on in here boy."

Even though I had to sleep on the couch it felt 100 times better than being in that cell. It wasn't until after everyone went to bed, when I finally began to wind down and get comfortable. I had to get back used to the silence. That didn't last for long, because Tiffany was up to her old tricks again. She Snuck out of her bedroom in the middle of the night and tried to get a quickie, but I blew her off. I told her straight up that I wasn't with it anymore, and it seemed to really rub her the wrong way. The next morning she acted like she didn't want to speak, and was getting short with me every time I asked her a question. She waited until Kelly went off to work, and Keke went off to school, to start an argument.

"What are you gonna do here all day?"

she asked.

"I'm gonna be leaving in a few minutes I got some things I gotta do."

"Like what? Look for a job?"

"Don't worry about it, I won't be asking you for nothing. I can pull my own weight."

"I hope you won't be doing any illegal shit, because if you do, you know you can't stay here."

"Who said anything about doing illegal shit?"

"I'm just saying, how else are you gonna get any money? You don't have any skills, no education, - nothing."

"You don't know what skills I have. And why are you bringing this up now? You knew about my situation before I even got out of jail. You're just mad about last night."

"This doesn't have anything to do with last night Robert! I'm just not gonna let you get us all kicked out of here behind your foolishness!"

"What foolishness? I haven't been out 48 hours and you're already accusing me of shit. All this drama because I don't want to fuck you anymore."

"Listen I don't need you for sex ok. You just ain't gonna be doing no illegal shit in my house."

"So I guess you screwing me isn't illegal huh? You know I'm only a minor, if I were to say something who would be in trouble, me or you?"

Tiffany raised her voice real loud and said,

"Are you gonna try and blackmail me now nigga? Is that what you're trying to do? Go ahead and try it Motherfucker and see what happens to you!"

I laughed and said, "What's gonna happen?"

I slowly walked towards her, until I was right up in her face.

She started to yell,

"Back up off me Robert! I'm telling you now, back up off me! Don't try and pull that jail shit with me!"

"What are you gonna do Tiffany? You make me back up!"

I had her pressed up against the kitchen sink; I was standing damn near nose to nose with her. She immediately reached back and grabbed a knife out of the dish rack, and plunged it into my left shoulder; just below my collar bone. I looked down and saw only the handle of the knife sticking out. The blade was completely inserted. My first thought was, why? - Why would she be so quick to stab me when I never laid a hand on her; ever. Instinctively my first reaction was to defend myself, and that's exactly what I did. I beat blood out this bitch with the knife still stuck in me. I pinned her down on her kitchen floor and pounded her face with my fists until the screaming stopped. She wasn't moving. Her eyes were swollen shut and pieces of her broken teeth were embedded in my knuckles. I knew she wasn't dead because I could hear her breathing, or should I say wheezing, through her broken nose. I stood up and slowly pulled the knife out of my shoulder. It went clean through just under the bone. It was less blood than I expected so I figured she didn't hit anything vital. I grabbed a towel out the bathroom to wrap my shoulder up, and then went looking around the apartment for something valuable that I could possibly sell. Everything I planned to do that day went right down the drain. I needed some quick cash to get the fuck out of dodge. I knew her jewelry wasn't worth shit; so I was hoping I'd find some cash in her purse to at least pay for a cab. I prayed that her neighbors didn't hear all the commotion and call the cops. But I didn't want to chance it, and got outta there ASAP.

This broke bitch had only 20 bucks in her purse. Enough to take me nowhere but back to prison on another aggravated robbery charge, so I just left it and quickly exited the apartment. I quietly closed the door behind me and sought of tip-toed down the hallway towards the elevator. I didn't hear any sirens going off outside so I figured I was cool... I just had to keep my cool. As I approached the elevator its doors opened and out came my mom, carrying a shopping bag full of clothes. Before she could say a word I put my index finger to my lips and motioned for her to be quiet. I gently grabbed her by her arm and escorted her back into the elevator. As we rode down she whispered,

"What's going on Robert? What happened?"

"I fucked Tiffany up Ma. I gotta get out of town."

"What?"

"We got in an argument, she stabbed me in the shoulder, and I blacked out on her. Now I gotta get the fuck outta dodge. How did you get here Ma? Did you drive or take the train?"

"Oh my God Robert, is she hurt bad?"

"Well she's not dead."

We exited the elevator in the lobby and headed out the front door. I saw the nervousness on my mom's face as we walked outside.

"I drove. My car is parked out back behind the building," She said.

We shuffled over to the car as fast as we could, without looking too obvious. We got in the car and drove off.

"Where are you gonna go Robert?"

"I don't know but I gotta get away from here."

"Well we won't get far in this car it's not in the best of shape. We gotta find another way to travel, but first we need to know where we're going to go."

With one hand on the steering wheel and the other massaging her chin, she breathed out the words,

"Let me think…"

"Ma … you can't go with me. If I get caught and we're together you'll be an accomplice and get locked up too. Don't forget, I'm already fighting a case."

"Do you really think Tiff is gonna press charges? What exactly did you do to her?"

"I messed her up bad ma. I knocked some of her teeth out, probably broke her nose, and who knows what else… Believe me, She's gonna press charges."

"Jesus Robert you just got out. What was y'all fighting about? You couldn't just walk away from her?"

"She fucking stabbed me ma! Walk away? There ain't no walking away from that."

"Let me see where she stab you at?"

I pulled off my shirt and showed her the wound.

"Damn it looks deep. Did you put anything on it?"

"Ma, when would I have had the time to put something on it? It all happened so fast and I had to get out of there with the quickness."

"I'll stop at a CVS or Walgreens to get some medicine and gauze to try and bandage you up, and then we'll go straight to the bus station. Maybe it's time that you got out of New York. Maybe go back to Cali… Visit your grandma or better yet, I should call your father and let him know that you need to spend some time with him now. I'll play it off and say that you're not listening to me anymore and that you need a male figure in your life to teach you how to be a man. You know, that same old single black mom song and dance."

"My father? C'mon ma I rather go to grandmas. I don't even know that nigga anymore."

"That's why it's best you go to him. Remember they gonna be looking for you, so grandma's house will be one of the first places they're gonna check. Your father on the other hand; I don't even have an address on that motherfucker, only a number. You don't have his last name, he's not on your birth certificate, and he's white. So that's who I think we should call."

My mom knows she can devise a plan. We went to Walgreens, picked up some meds, then drove to the Port Authority bus terminal.

After we finally found somewhere to park, she patched me up the best she could, then we went inside. I was paranoid as hell. Every police officer and security guard I passed I looked at suspiciously. And I bet they weren't even thinking about me. My mom purchased the ticket on her credit card then got on the pay phone to call my long lost dad. I took a seat, rested my head between my folded arms on the back of the chair that was in front of me, and stared at the floor. The adrenaline was starting to wear off, and my shoulder was really starting to hurt. I glanced over at my mom chatting on the phone and saw her violently hang up the receiver. A look of frustration was written on her face as she walked over to where I was. But she spoke as if everything was cool.

"He'll be there to pick you up when you get there," she said.

"Why did you hang up the phone like that Ma?"

"Oh it was nothing. He was just saying how he missed me, and asked if I was coming with you. I just wasn't in the mood to hear his bullshit, that's why I hung up on him."

"Did you tell him what happened?"

"No I told him exactly what I told you I would say when we were in the car. The only thing different that I said, was that you got in a little trouble. So I'll leave it up to you if you wanna tell him anything else when you get there. But I would advise you not. You need to just lay low, see if he can get you back in school or get a job or something until this thing blows over. I'm gonna try and reach out to Tiff if I can, and try and convince her to drop the charges. I might have to pay her."

"Pay her?" Nah… Ma I need to tell you something."

"What?"

"I was really trying to avoid telling you this but now you're talking about paying her off, and I can't let that happen without you knowing."

"Knowing what? - Go ahead say what you gotta say. What is it?"

"You ain't gonna like it."

"What do you gotta tell me? Boy, come on."

"Dam Ma I'm ashamed to say it, but, I've been fucking Tiffany for a while now. I mean, It was before I got locked up."

The look on her face completely changed. An angry scowl transformed her otherwise subtle looking mug, to something ugly. She shook her head, and took a deep breath before uttering,

"I knew something was up with her that night at the hospital. Acting a fool when I said you couldn't come over her house anymore. I can see if it was Keke you were messing around with; but Tiffany, that bitch is my age! Robert, why?"

"I don't know it just sort of happened. But I told her that I wanted to end it and that's how the whole fight started."

"And I thought that hoe was a lesbian. Does Kelly know about this? Now I know why she was so eager for you to come stay with her. She didn't even wanna take my money to help out with the rent. Saying she was offended that I offered her money, that you're her Godson, and we were family. Oooh, that trifling bitch! I trusted her. You know what Robert, don't say nothing else. Just get ready to hop your ass on that bus so you get the fuck up out of here!"

We sat there for over an hour without saying a word to each other. It was finally time for me to board…

"Bye ma."

7 "DEALING WITH BACKSTABBERS, THERE WAS ONE THING I LEARNED. THEY'RE ONLY POWERFUL WHEN YOU GOT YOUR BACK TURNED." - EMINEM

I saw my mom's reflection bounce off the glass of the bus window. Her back was facing me so I tapped on the window to try and get her attention; but she didn't turn around. As the bus began to pull away, my tapping got louder. I started to bang on the window so hard with my hand, I was scared it was going to crack. All I wanted to do was wave my final goodbye, but it seemed like she was ignoring me on purpose. The hood from her jacket was pulled down over her head, and she had her hands covering her face. I didn't realize it at the time, but she was crying.

As soon as she got back to her car, she

began to reapply her makeup, and she laid it on thick. Reason being she was trying to cover up all the little scars she'd got from her many fights with Milford. Not only that; she was preparing her face for the confrontation she expected to have with Tiffany. There was no doubt that it was going to end in a fight.

She tied her sneakers up tight, and pulled her hair back into a ponytail. All of that extra makeup she put on was to give her face a little protection, since she didn't have any Vaseline.

She drove back over to Tiffany's residence and parked out in front of the building. Her intuition told her to call first before going inside, and she followed her gut feeling.

The telephone rang three times before anyone answered.

"Hello?"

Charlene, trying her best to be pleasant answered, "Hey who's this?"

"It's Keke."

"Hey baby girl it's Charlene, I didn't recognize your voice. Is your mom home?"

"Yeah hold on." *(In the background Keke could be overheard saying)* "Ma, Miss Charlene is on the phone."

Charlene was trying to stay calm and pretend like she didn't know about the fight or the affair. But she thought it was odd the way Keke answered the phone. If her mom was beaten up in the way that it was described to her, why would Keke act like everything was normal. She seemed mighty chipper.

Tiffany picked up the phone and said, "Hey Charlene what's up?"

"Hey Tiff what's going on?"

"Nothing, I'm just straightening up, and I was about to cook dinner."

Puzzled, and at a little loss for words, Charlene decided to throw a hook out there to see what she would catch.

"Is Robert there?"

Tiffany hesitantly answered, "Nah girl he left early this morning and he's been gone all day... I know you were gonna bring him some clothes and stuff. You haven't seen him?"

"No I haven't. Hmmm... I don't know what that boy is up to. But how are you? Are you catching a cold? You sound stopped up."

"Nah girl," (*she chuckled*) "You ain't gonna believe this. I was carrying my laundry basket down stairs to do some laundry, and tripped and hit my face on the edge of the door."

Acting as if she was concerned Charlene replied, "Oh no… are you okay?"

"Well I busted my nose and cracked a couple of teeth. My eyes are a little swollen but I'm good."

"You busted your nose? Did you go to the hospital or see a doctor? Charlene asked.

"Nah I kinda pushed it back into place myself, and stuffed it with cotton to stop the bleeding."

Giggling, Charlene replied, "Oh my God, you gotta be careful... What else did you say happened? You chipped or broke your tooth?… dam!"

"Yeah girl, they weren't real any way. Keke's dad and I use to fight all the time, and he knocked out some of my real teeth. I went to the dentist and he put in a bridge. But I got the new style shit where you don't see the metal hooks so no one can tell. You know what I'm saying?"

Charlene, trying really hard now to hold back the laughs said, "Girl you crazy, I'm just glad you're all right."

"Yeah I'm cool. I got an emergency

appointment tomorrow with my dentist, and he'll hook me up with a new one. Right now I'm looking crazy. I got teeth missing right in the front, but I'll be back looking fly by tomorrow."

Charlene couldn't hold it off any longer and started laughing hysterically. Not because she thought it was funny; it was her way of relieving the anxiety that she had built up before making the call. She didn't know how the conversation was gonna go, but she felt a lot better knowing that Tiffany was gonna roll with this story even though it was a lie.

After her whimsical outburst they continued on with the conversation, but there was a noticeable change in Tiffany's demeanor. It was more down-beat, almost as if someone knocked the wind out of her.

"Where are you now Charlene?" Tiffany asked.

"I'm in the car... just cruising around..."

Charlene could tell something was wrong by the sudden change in Tiffany's voice, so she tried to smooth it out.

"Oh girl I'm sorry. Did I hurt your feelings? I didn't mean to laugh. It's just the way you were explaining it. I'm sorry. But yeah I'm in the car heading home. Why?"

"Oh, no reason, I was just looking out my bedroom window and I saw a car that looked like yours parked across the street from my building, that's all. Just thought that if you were in the neighborhood, why didn't you come up?"

"Nah girl I'm about to turn down my block right now."

Tiffany observed the headlights on Charlene's car turn on. She kept an eye on it as it pulled away from the parking spot. She knew that it was Charlene by the red scarf that was wrapped around her neck. She had given her that scarf a few years ago as a Christmas gift, and she wore it all the time.

To confirm it she asked, "Did it get chilly out? I was outside earlier and it was kinda nice. If I go out again, how should I dress? Do you think I need a coat?"

"Yeah the temperature dropped. I got on my heavy jacket and a scarf. So you better bundle up."

"I know you ain't still rocking that scarf I bought you like 3 years ago?"

"You know it. That's my favorite scarf."

Tiffany nodded her head as if to say I caught you, you lying bitch, but she continued to play along.

"Okay, now I know to grab my coat when I go out. I think I'm gonna run to the corner store before they close. I'll tell Robert to call you when he gets in, Cool?"

"All right… talk to you later, bye."

They both hung up.

Tiffany continued to stare out the window, thoroughly convinced now that Charlene knew what really happened between her and Robert, and that she only called to seek out information; like did she go to the cops, or was she planning on pressing charges.

Keke ran into the room and broke Tiffany's chain of thought.

"Ma what are you staring at? Who's outside?"

"Nobody Keke I was just... Sit down for a minute I need to tell you something."

"okay ma Girlfriends is about to come on. I don't wanna miss it, so make it quick."

"Okay, sit down."

Tiffany pats the bed instructing her where to sit.

"You know the story I told you earlier on how I got hurt? Well… It wasn't exactly true. Shit, it wasn't true at all."

"So how did it happen ma?"

"Robert did this to me… He beat my ass."

Keke was in total shock. All she could do was sit there with her mouth wide open and continue to listen.

"I'm planning on pressing charges. I was gonna handle it myself and not go to the Police, but I changed my mind. He gotta learn his lesson the hard way."

"What the hell happened ma? Did you tell Charlene? What did she say?" Keke asked.

"Nah I didn't tell her."

"Why?"

Tiffany didn't immediately answer. Instead, she began to fiddle around her room and look through old mail that was scattered about on her dresser. Completely ignoring the question.

"Why ma? Why didn't you tell Charlene? You're gonna go straight to the cops without even telling her what happened?"

"There's things you don't know about Charlene. She's not as nice as you think she is Keke."

"But what does that have to do with anything?… What were you and Robert fighting about anyway?"

"It's a long story, but If you see him out in the street stay away from him. Don't even talk to him. he's no good."

"Ma, he was just living here with us. Now you want me to stay away from him? What changed all of a sudden? You were dying for him to stay, and now you don't want him around. You did the same thing with daddy! … I guess you really have a problem with guys!"

"So you're gonna take up for him and totally disregard what happened to me? Look at my face. Do you see what he did to me?"

"I'm not taking up for him! You won't tell me what happened. You don't wanna tell Charlene. Does Kelly know? Did you tell her?"

"No. I'll tell her when she gets home from work, but I'm surprised at you. I'm really surprised that you would go against your own mother for some… you know what Keke go. You can leave now. Go ahead; go watch Girlfriends or whatever the fuck it is you wanna see on t.v."

"Ma really?… You gonna act like that?"

"Go ahead Keke get out! I don't wanna talk no more!"

Keke threw her hands up in the air, turned around and marched out the room. Tiffany angrily slammed the door behind her. They didn't speak for the rest of the evening.

A couple of miles away, Charlene was pulling up in front of her dimly lit, ranch styled home, that she shared with Milford. She threw the car in park, turned off the lights, but left the engine idling. She sat there and thought about the conversation she just had with Tiffany; now wishing that she would've confronted her about everything instead of playing ignorant. There was still time, but at that moment she was more in the mood to spark up a blunt, lay back in the seat and unwind. She really wasn't a smoker, but she always kept a small bag of weed in her purse for special occasions. This would be considered one of those occasions.

Like always, when things start to get good, there's always something or someone to blow your high. This time it happened to be Milford, who was knocking on the driver's side window. Charlene put her partially lit blunt out, and rolled the window down half way.

"Hey, what's up?"

Milford angrily replied, "Why are you sitting out here in the dark? And where you been all day?

"I just pulled up not even 5 minutes ago; can you give me a chance to get out the car?"

She turned the engine off, pulled the key out the ignition, and grabbed her pocketbook.

"Are you gonna move so I can open the door?"

Milford slid over to the side as she exited the car; staring at her the whole time. His eyes didn't even blink, and she refused to make eye contact with him.

"You didn't answer my question," Milford mumbled.

"What Milford?... What?... Why you wanna start? You always wanna argue."

"I asked you a question. Where have you been all day?"

"Out, I was out running errands... Okay? Is that ok with you?"

"Why you getting all snippy with me? You probably was out with your nigga. That's where you probably was. Just don't bring his ass back around here."

Disgusted, Charlene replied, "What the fuck are you talking about?"

"Your nigga Robert, that's what I'm talking about."

Charlene walked around the back of the car and onto the sidewalk. She paused for a moment and said,

"Why are you always sweating him? You got issues… And get it straight motherfucker, he's my son and not some nigga."

Milford leaned against her car, grabbed his crotch and yelled, "I didn't say some nigga, I said YOUR NIGGA! You act like he's your nigga instead of your son. I wouldn't be surprised if you were giving him the pussy."

"You know what, I'm not even gonna respond to that. You've been jealous of my son since we met. I don't know what it is. Maybe your mama didn't show you enough attention growing up, or Robert reminds you of someone from your childhood that you wanted to be like. But I had enough of your shit. I'm gonna go inside get a couple of my things and I'm bouncing. I'll come back for the rest of my stuff later. There ain't no hard feelings and I hope you have a nice life."

Milford stood there silent while she continued to walk toward the front of the house. When she got to the door, she nervously looked back to see where he was. He was standing in the same spot next to her car, and was still staring at her.

"I bet his fat ass is gonna try and do something to my car," she whispered.

So with no delay she quickly grabbed a few of her necessary items, threw them in a trash bag and called it a day.

She slowly opened the front door, just enough to peek out. Milford was no longer standing by the car. In fact, there was no sign of him at all. Assuming that the coast was clear she tip-toed out of the house, and made a b-line to her car. She hopped in, turned the key in the ignition, and nothing happened.

"Maybe you should check your battery."

She quickly turned around and saw Milford sitting in the backseat. Before she had a chance to react; he slapped her in her face so hard that her head hit the side window, shattered the glass, and knocked her unconscious.

Trust & Believe

8 "THE QUESTION IS WHAT I WANTED TO DO WITH THE NEW LIFE GOD HAS GIVEN ME. THIS IS THE MISSION I WANT TO TAKE ON." - BILLY TAUZIN

I couldn't do it. I couldn't go off and leave my mom with the burden of trying to straighten out my problems once again. I struggled with the idea from the very moment that I boarded the bus, and came to the conclusion that I should've gotten off two or three stops earlier, instead of staying on all the way to Pennsylvania. Harrisburg to be exact.

I barely had enough cash to buy a ticket from there, back to New York; and after I did, I had to wait nearly two hours for the next bus to come. By the time I returned to Manhattan, it was a little after midnight, and the whole area around the Port Authority bus and subway stations were swarming with cops.

My plan of hopping the train home went right out the window. I was too scared to jump the turnstile with all of those cops around, and I didn't have any funds left to pay the fare. Maybe I had thirty-five cents, if that, to my name. I probably could've bummed the rest of the money off of somebody, but I didn't want to bring unnecessary attention to myself.

That's when homeboy crossed my mind. I'm talking about Taps.

I figured that he'd probably be the only person I could call right then and there, to help me out. So I took that little bit of change that I had, and used it to call him.

I took a deep breath, dialed his number, and hoped that he would answer the phone. When no one answered after the fourth ring, I started to get a little worried.

"Is he gonna pick up or what. This pay phone better not keep my money if he doesn't pick up. Come on Taps, come on answer the fucking phone," I whispered.

After about the sixth or seventh ring a woman with a very hoarse sounding voice, finally answered.

"Hello!"

"Hi, may I speak with Taps, I mean, Sammy please?"

"Who is this?"

"Umm, my name is Robert. I'm a classmate of his. I just wanted to ask him a question about our homework."

"At this time of night? Do you realize what time it is?"

"Umm... I kinda lost track of time. I got stuck trying to figure out this problem, and I wanted to see if Sammy could help me out."

"What's the problem?"

"Huh?"

"What's the problem you're trying to figure out? I'm a teacher, I probably can help."

"Well, it's umm, like a math problem and..."

In the background I could hear Tap's voice asking,

"Who are you talking to ma?"

"It's one of your pals from school," she replied.

I assumed that he must of snatched the phone out of her hand by the way she shouted, "Well excuse you Sammy, you don't have to be so rude!"

"Hello who's this?" Taps asked.

"Yo this is Robert. Was that your mom?"

"Yeah, but don't mind her, she's off her meds. What's going on bro? Long time no hear."

"I'm cool. First off I wanna thank you for looking out. If it wasn't for you I'd still be locked up. So whatever you need I got you. No questions asked. But I need one more favor from you B. I'm stuck at the Port Authority and don't have enough dough to get home."

"You don't need no money, just jump the turnstile."

"It's mad cops out here tonight, and remember I'm out on bail. If they catch me I'm not getting a D. A. T. I'm going straight to jail. Plus I got into some other shit earlier and I don't know if they're looking for me for that. I'm fucked up right now."

"Dam didn't you just get out a day or so ago, and you're already getting into shit?"

"Yo B, shit happens. I don't know what to tell you."

"It's cool, but hey umm, how's she doing?"

"Who?"

"Your mom."

"Oh, she's chillin."

"Did she say anything?"

"What you mean? Say anything about what?"

"About me."

I paused for a moment to think about what he asked. He kinda sounded anxious to hear what I had to say, so I thought I'd mess with him a little bit.

"Yeah, she said you was hot, and if you were older she'd probably date you."

He got real silent.

"I'm playing. Nah man, she didn't say nothing, but believe me, she does appreciate you helping us out. Why? Was there something you wanted her to tell me?"

"No bro it's nothing, forget about it."

"So yo, my time is about to run out on this phone; I need you to pick me up. Can you do it? Or do you have to ask your moms for permission?"

"I don't have to ask my mom for shit. Be on the corner of 42nd and 8th in an hour, and look out for my car."

"An hour? That long? I'm just playing. Good looking out B."

I didn't wait inside the station for Taps to get there; the cops had me too paranoid. I hit the street. My shoulder still hurt like hell, but when I saw all the different hoes walking around in that area, it eased the pain. Boy oh boy they were out there that night. And one in particular caught my eye. She had on red spandex pants, a glittery silver top, and her ass was humongous. Her face was kinda fucked up though. All broken out, probably from wearing that cheap dollar store makeup. But I won't even lie, if I had the money, I would've paid for that booty in a heartbeat.

I watched her walk the stroll for at least 45 minutes and surprisingly no one stopped to pick her up. Her compadres on the other hand, were getting plenty of business; both foot and vehicle traffic.

Every couple of minutes a car door would open and some hoe would spit cum out her mouth, or toss a used condom onto the ground. Eventually, someone did drive up and pull over by her, and for some strange reason I got a little upset. I don't know if I was jealous that I couldn't afford her and who ever this guy was could, or I was simply hating for no reason. Whatever the case I wasn't going to let it go down.

I tried my best to cross the street and get over to where she was, but there was so much traffic I couldn't cross right away. I kept my eyes on her though. And from my vantage point, I could see her lean into the car, have a few words with the guy, then storm off. My first thought was that maybe he didn't wanna pay her what she wanted, and she got mad and walked away. I realized that I was wrong when the guy got out of his car, presumably to go after her, but began to wave in my direction.

I was lusting after that hoe so bad that I didn't realize that it was Taps. When I was finally able to cross the street, I walked up to him, shook his hand and said,

"Sorry B, but that hoe over there had me in a trance."

"Who? The one that came up to my car with all the bumps on her face?"

"Fuck her face, look at that ass…"

"I prefer a big tittied chick myself, but to each his own," Taps explained.

"Ha, you're bugging B!"

We both chuckled as we got in his car. Still, I couldn't keep my eyes off of that hoe. And now since I was closer, I could see her a whole lot better. She was a bit older than I thought. She looked like she could have been around my mom's age, but it didn't make a difference to me. I thought that she was hot to death, fucked up face and all. The more I stared at her the more familiar she began to look. I turned to taps and said, "Yo she look mad familiar B, I know her from somewhere."

"You still sweating that chick? You wanna bang her don't you?"

"Hell yeah! I would tear that ass up, but she probably want a lot of money."

"A lot of money? I wouldn't give that bitch no more than 20 bucks. Tell her you got $20.00, don't worry I'll front you the money. I'll betcha she'll take it."

"I don't know Taps man; I don't wanna disrespect her."

"Disrespect her? Look what she's out here doing and your worried about disrespecting her. You gonna ask her or what?"

"Nah man, go ahead."

Taps put on his seatbelt and began to peer into his side view mirror, waiting for the opportunity to bust a u-turn. I still had my eye on the chick, and kept debating whether or not if I should take his advice and see if she'd let me hit it for $20. Suddenly she started to walk back over toward the car, just as we were pulling off.

"Hold up B, Hold up! She's coming back this way. I'm gonna ask her."

I leaned out the window as she walked up.

"What's up, how you doing Miss Lady?"

"Hey baby, I'm fine. What you getting into tonight? You want some company?"

"It all depends. I don't know if I can afford you."

Taps shook his head in disgust.

"Well how much you got?"

"I only got a dub."

"A dub? What the hell is a dub?"

"Twenty, twenty dollars."

"Oh ok. When you said a dub I was like, is this guy talking about drugs or something? Cause I don't do no drugs."

Taps voice echoed in from the background, "Yeah right."

She didn't hear him though, and continued on with her spiel.

"So I guess that's slang for $20.00 huh?" She chuckled. "I can work with 20."

Taps gave me a look like; I told you so.

"What you want, some head, or some ass?" she asked.

"Can I get both?"

"No sugar. For 20 you can only get one or

the other. Normally I wouldn't give up the ass for $20.00, but I think you're cute."

"Okay, I want some ass then."

"Is your friend gonna watch or participate? Cause he's gonna need $20 too, if he wants to fuck. I don't give discounts. When I came by earlier he was acting all scared and shit. He jumped out the car and started waving at you. I thought he was a homo."

I looked over at Taps with a smile and asked,

"What you gonna do Taps, participate? Or do you just wanna see me in action?"

"No thanks I'll pass on both!... And bitch I'm not a homo. Tell me, how many dicks have you sucked tonight?!"

"Taps chill!"

"Well excuse me! I see your friend is real sensitive. Just like a woman, and he got the nerve to call me a bitch."

"Robert, fuck this hoe lets go!"

"Taps chill for a minute... Just take us up a couple of blocks to 11th ave. Let me do my thing and then we can bounce. Yo B just do me this solid..."

I got out the car and opened the back door.

"Hey love, get in and slide over, I'm gonna sit back here with you."

Taps was angry but he agreed. He slid me the money without the hoe seeing it and I hopped in the backseat next to her. As we drove Taps kept looking back at us through his rear view. The hoe noticed him looking and began sticking her tongue out at him and making funny faces. I laughed, but It enraged him even more. When we got to 11th ave he made a quick right turn, swerved over to the curb and threw it in park. He didn't say a word, he just turned around and stared at her. She looked at me, then looked at him and said,

"What's your problem? Am I supposed to be scared? Fuck you! Let me out of this car."

"Come on Taps see what you did? Miss Lady don't go..." I said.

"You little boys out here trying to do grown men things, but y'all gotta lot of growing up to do. Especially you!"

She pointed her finger at Taps, then looked at me and said,

"I was gonna rock your world tonight. Make you feel like a man, but your boy fucked it up for you."

She got out the car and slammed the door.

"Good riddance," Taps said. "Let that stank hoe go. That bitch ain't even worth $20.00. I'm glad you didn't have to spend the money."

"Yo B, I gave her the money."

"You gave her the money? For what? She didn't even do anything other than make my car smell like fish! Fuck that, I'm getting my money back!"

Taps jumped out the car and started screaming at the hoe.

"Hey!... Hey!... Bitch don't walk away, slow down! Give me back my money!"

She turned to him and said,

"What are you talking about? I don't owe you no money. I didn't do any business with you!"

"The money he gave you, (he gestured back at the car) that's my money; and you didn't do nothing to earn it!"

"Didn't do nothing to earn it? You sound like a fool. Just entertaining your funny looking ass is reason enough to keep it. In fact you need to pay me 20 more dollars for wasting my time. Time is money, and I don't give refunds honey!"

"Oh yeah, bitch you're gonna give me back my money!" Taps screamed.

I watched the whole scene play out from the backseat of the car, and wondered why would he go crazy over $20.00, especially when he's not really hurting for it. They were standing damn near toe to toe, screaming at the top of their lungs at each other. At first; I thought it was funny seeing this bitch, who was fairly tall and towered over Taps, look like a parent scolding her child. She was pointing her finger in his face, and kept calling him a little boy. But suddenly everything went left. I saw Taps reach back into his waistband, pull out a little stick of some sort, then flail it downward; making it expand. Before I could jump out the car or yell stop, he had already whacked the hoe over her head with it, and she instantly dropped to the ground.

I quickly ran over to where they were. She was lying on the ground unconscious, and blood was gushing from her head. It didn't look like all the damage came from what he hit her with, it seemed like it came from the impact of her head hitting the sidewalk. Instead of checking to see how bad she was hurt, Taps had already started rummaging through her purse for the $20.

"What the hell is wrong with you B?...

Are you crazy? Yo, I don't think she's breathing," I said.

Both of us looked around to see if anybody was in the area, and as strange as it may seem, there was no one in sight. Taps lifted her shirt and reached down in her bra, still in search of the money; but it was to no avail. He then slid his hand down her pants, and wound up finding her hidden stash tucked in her G-string.

"Bingo!" He shouted.

Then he began to count it out and it came to be a little over 200 bucks. He handed me half of the money, and put the other half in his pocket.

"Alright lets go," he whispered.

"Wait, what you mean lets go? What about her?" I said.

"What about her?

"We can't just leave her here like this."

"Why not? This is New York City. They find dead hoes around here everyday."

"How you know she's dead?"

"Didn't you just say she wasn't breathing?"

"Yeah, I mean… I'm not a doctor B. It looked like she wasn't breathing. Did you check her?"

Taps put his hand in front of her nose, then put his head on her chest.

"Nope. She's not breathing."

"Oh shit man! We got to at least call an ambulance or drop her off at the hospital or something."

"The fuck we are! We're leaving her ass right here. We're not calling the cops, a ambulance, or nothing! You must really like jail, cause that's where we're going if we say anything about this."

"But there's evidence. You just had your hands all over her."

"I really don't think the cops will waste their resources doing a thorough investigation on her. A white hoe maybe, but a black one… negative."

"That's some fucked up shit to say B."

"It's the truth! But to be on the safe side; I got a jug of antifreeze and some rags in the trunk. We can wipe her down with that. Antifreeze has alcohol in it and that should get rid of any fingerprints or DNA."

I stared at him for a moment and thought, who the fuck is this guy? From the short time that I've known him I figured he was just some goofy white boy trying to be down; but now I saw him in a whole different light. He's on some other shit! And I had no choice but to follow his lead.

We dragged her by her feet over to the side of his car, stripped her naked, and wiped her body down with the antifreeze. My heart was beating a mile a minute. I was working so hard and moving so fast that the bandages on my shoulder became undone, and I started to bleed through my shirt. Taps on the other hand didn't break a sweat. He was whistling and humming the theme song to that old TV show, 'MASH', the whole entire time.

We left her there naked on the side of the road, and threw her clothes in a random dumpster on our way back to Queens.

During the ride I couldn't even look at him. He kept trying to lighten the mood by cracking jokes, but I didn't find nothing he was saying funny. I felt indebted to this nigga now. We both had something to hold over each others head, but the weight on my shoulders felt heavier.

9 "WHEN WE DIE, OUR SOULS STILL LIVE. IF YOU ARE A GANGSTER OR A BASTARD OR A CROOK, YOUR SOUL INHABITS A DONKEY OR SOMETHING TERRIBLE." - MOHAMED AL-FAYED

She was awakened by someone repeatedly banging on the front door of their house. She rolled off of the couch and onto the living room floor, crawled on all fours to an end table, then hoisted herself up onto her feet. The bright morning sunlight that beamed through the transom window, caused her eyes to squint, and it also magnified the painful headache that she woke up with. She saw the outline of two men standing outside of her home. She glanced over at the clock on the wall, and figured that it couldn't be no one else but the police, that was banging on the door that early in the morning. If they were looking for Milford he was gone. He did what he normally does; and that is slip out the back door, just as they arrive at the front. The last thing she remembered was him popping up in the backseat of her car, smacking the shit out of her, and barely nothing else.

She couldn't recall if she was the one who called the police, or if a neighbor did, like they often do, when she and him have their disputes. So she optimistically answered the door not knowing what to expect.

It was two detectives that greeted her. They had their badges in hand, and a hard stare plastered across their faces. There was no doubt that they noticed her swollen jaw and black eye, but ignored it and got right to the business at hand.

"Is Robert here?" One officer asked.

She was confused by the question. Thinking, why would they be asking for Robert, instead of Milford.

"No he isn't," She replied.

"What's your relation to him?"

"I'm his mother, Charlene."

"We got this address from his bondsman ma'am, all we want to do is talk to him."

"Well he's not here officer."

"Do you know where he is?"

"Umm… I think he left for school."

"This early in the morning?"

"Umm… yeah. He stops by his friends house and they walk to school together."

"So he's already back in school? He just got out of jail the other day… Hmmm… that was quick," the detective sarcastically said.

"What's his Friend's name?"
His partner asked.

"It's umm… Tommy… or Tyrone… one of them, I'm not sure."

"Not sure huh?… Did Robert do that to your face?"

"Of course not!… Never! What is this all about officer?"

"We just need to speak with him. It's important. Here's my card. When you get in contact with him give us a call."

Charlene nodded her head, took the card, and closed the door. She continued to look out the window as the detectives walked back to their car. Unable to make out what they were saying, she could only watch them shake their heads and make hand gestures as they conversed with each other.

"That bitch is lying," one detective said, as he threw his hands in the air.

"I know, but they continue to protect these little bastards," said the other.

"I bet he's the one that beat the crap out of her. The injuries are similar to the complainant's. I wouldn't be surprised if he did; these people have a sick sense of values."

No sooner than five minutes after the officers got in their car and drove away; that Milford came strolling up. He had apparently been watching from somewhere nearby and waited till the coast was clear before he returned home. And like usual, a bouquet of gas station flowers was in his hand. He came inside and put the flowers down on a coffee table, right smack in front of Charlene.

"I'm sorry baby. I don't know what got into me last night. I've been going through a lot on the job, and I know I shouldn't be taking it out on you."

Charlene didn't say a word.

"You gotta understand, I'm trying to protect you. When you come home late and don't call to let me know that you're gonna be late, I worry. This ain't exactly the best neighborhood. I don't know why you like to sit in your car outside of the house, instead of coming in. That's dangerous. You could get jacked or even shot by one of these knuckleheads around here."

She remained silent, as he tried to justify the reason for beating her up.

"And your son,… I don't wanna keep talking about your son, but, you gotta realize he ain't shit. Excuse my French. But you keep protecting him. Now you're bailing him out of jail. I bet you didn't think I knew that did you? I got people out here in these streets. You can't hide nothing from me. I ain't even gonna ask you where you got the money from; just as long as you don't mess with my money, we're cool. But he's gonna be your downfall. For real!"

Charlene continued to bite her tongue, as he pranced back and forth in front of her, rambling mindlessly. She started to focus in on a cast iron skillet, resting on top of the stove. She thought if she timed it right she could run, grab the skillet, and knock him over the head with it before he knew what hit him. She was trying real hard to drum up the nerve. The more he went on, the angrier she got. It came to a point where she had had enough, and was willing to take the chance.

On the count of three she was gonna make her move.

The countdown in her head began. One Mississippi, two Mississippi, three! Her cell phone rang at the exact same time of her three count, and inadvertently drew her attention from the skillet on the stove, to her phone on the coffee table. It caught Milford off guard. He nervously jumped and guarded himself with his hands when she suddenly darted across the room to get it.

"What the fuck?... You're breaking your neck just to get to the phone?"

She ignored him and answered the call.

"Hello?"

"Aye ma!"

Instinctively Charlene turned her back to Milford, moved a few steps further away from him, and began to whisper.

"Hey Robert, where are you? Everything okay?"

"Yeah I'm okay ma, but I'm back."

"Back? Back where?"

"Back here in New York. I'm back in the Rockaways. I'm at Taps crib. But listen before you get upset, let me explain. I can't let you keep fighting my battles. It's time that I deal with my own shit, and not brush it off on you. In fact, I should be helping you out."

Glancing back over her shoulder, Charlene saw the anger building on Milford's face, and immediately interrupted.

"Robert listen I can't talk right now, can I reach you at this number?"

"Why? Is he there? Is he fucking with you again ma?"

"I'll call you back Robert. Please, let me call you back."

Before she could say goodbye, Milford had made a move toward her and attempted to snatch the phone out of her hand.

"What's with all the whispering and shit?!" he yelled. "Why you gotta do everything so sneaky? I'm getting sick and tired of it! And you wonder why you're always getting your ass beat!"

Charlene held the phone up over her head, and tried to angle it away from him.

A tussle ensued.

There was a lot of rumbling, grunting, and finally a loud scream echoed through the phone before the call disconnected.

"Ma!, Ma! You there? What's going

on?"

A strange sinking feeling moved through my stomach. I looked over at Taps who was present when I made the call, and told him that I had to head to my mom's crib to take care of some business. He volunteered to roll with me, so we jumped in his car and bounced.

"Get your fat ass off me!" Charlene screamed.

Milford had tackled her onto the floor, and pinned both of her arms over her head.

"Give me the mother-fucking phone bitch," he said as he snatched it out of her hand.

He leant back, sat on her stomach, and squinted his eyes trying to focus in on the screen. Using his index finger, he began to scroll through the names and numbers of all her recent calls.

"Who were you talking to? Who the fuck is Irving Singer? Huh? Who is he?"

Charlene tried desperately to push him off, but only had enough energy left to belt out the words, "I can't breathe!" While she simultaneously pounded on his chest.

"So you're not gonna answer me huh?"

Milford momentarily stared at the

phone, then stood up and proceeded to dial the last incoming call; which happened to be Tap's parents home number.

"Yeah, your ass thought you was slick but you got caught," he mumbled.

Tap's mom picked up after the first ring, and in a cheerful voice she answered,

"Good morning."

"Who's this?" Milford asked.

"This is Joan, and whom may I ask am I speaking to?"

"Yo who the fuck is Irving?"

"Sir! Your language please! My gosh, Irving is my husband. Who am I speaking to please?"

Sounding agitated Milford replied, "Why is your husband calling my girl lady? If you love him, you better tell him to leave her alone. He better not call this number again!"

Tap's mom began to shake. Unsure of what to say, she hesitated before responding to the accusations.

"Who's your girlfriend? What's her name? Wait… it really doesn't matter. Sir I believe you're mistaken. My husband doesn't have a reason to call her, or any other woman. If I understand what you're getting at, he would never partake in such foolishness. We've been married for over 20 years, and he'd never do such a thing."

"Well I'm telling you lady, he did that shit! And when I see him I'm gonna put my foot in his ass!"

Charlene tried to grab the phone back out of Milford's hand, and another struggle ensued. Once again, he was victorious. He pushed her against a wall, and knocked a mirror loose, causing it to crash down over her head. During the struggle the phone was unintentionally hung up, but Tap's mom heard some of what was going on before she got cut off.

"Sir, sir, oh lord what are you doing to that woman?! I'm gonna call the police! Irving come quick! Irving, Irving, do you hear me calling you Irving!"

"What Joan? What? What do you want?"

"Come down stairs right now, Hurry!"

"What is it? What's so important that you can't wait till I get out of bed to tell me? What the hell time is it?!"

"Don't worry about what time it is Irving! I need you down here now!"

"Oy vey! Alright give me a minute, I'll

be right down."

10 "ANYBODY WHO THINKS TALK IS CHEAP SHOULD GET SOME LEGAL ADVICE." - FRANKLIN P. JONES

I rolled up to my mom's crib, prepared and ready for action. I told Taps to wait in the car and that I'd holla if I needed him. Armed with only a box cutter, I was confident that I could take care of business. This wasn't gonna be a repeat of the last time.

I heard the yelling as soon as I got out of the car. All that racket had to have woken up a few of the neighbors. I definitely knew for sure that it woke up at least one. I caught her peeking through her blinds, but she quickly closed them after I spotted her. I figured it would only be a matter of minutes before the cops got there, because that neighbor in particular, was always calling them.

I was trying to decide if I should knock, or just kick the door in. As I stood in front of it debating, it suddenly flew open, and out came my mom, cussing and screaming at the top of her lungs.

Running behind her, looking like King Kong, was fat boy Milford. He had gotten even bigger since the last time I saw him. Mostly in his belly. When he saw me, he stopped dead in his tracks. He was holding a cell phone in one hand and a broken broomstick in the other.

My mom had jetted passed me and made her way out to the street. She posted up behind a vehicle, and continued to hurl insults at him. I'm not sure if she even realized that it was me that she just ran past.

Milford had shifted his attention off of her, and directed it towards me. In doing so, he attempted to hit me across the head with the broomstick; but I saw it coming and moved out of the way. I whipped out the razor that was in my back pocket, and got to slicing.

"Yeah nigga, take that!" I yelled, as I slid it down his face.

I caught him at the base of his right ear, and brought it down to the corner of his top lip. That didn't stop him though, he continued to swing wildly with that broomstick; but hit nothing but air. I jabbed at him again, and slit his forearm. That one slowed him up a bit, and he stepped back. I didn't think he realized he was cut, until he saw all the blood running down his arm. His face for some reason wasn't bleeding. Only a whelp appeared. But as soon as he wiped his face with his hand, that's when that shit opened up.

"Oh shit you cut my face! Nigga I'm a kill you!" He screamed.

I jumped down off of the steps and into the weed patch in the front yard. He turned around and ran back inside the house.

"He's probably going to get his gun," my mom yelled.

Taps had just gotten out of his car, but quickly hopped back in, when he heard the word gun. He didn't even wait for me. He started it up, and took off.

I ran out of the yard, forcibly grabbed my mom by the arm, and had to practically drag her away from the front of the house.

"C'mon ma, we gotta get outta here."

But for some odd reason she wanted to stay there and agitate him even more.

"He ain't crazy. He don't have the heart to shoot nobody. He's just trying to scare you. You see what happened when you fought back right? He turned around and ran. All he is, is a woman beater, that's all he is!" she yelled.

We made it about 20 paces from the house, then heard boom boom boom, in a rapid succession. That motherfucker was shooting at us. But like with the broomstick, he didn't hit nothing; at least I thought, until I saw my mom topple over. One minute she was jogging alongside of me, the next minute she's on the ground.

Trying to stay low, I pulled her out of the street, and behind some bushes in one of the neighbor's yards.

Then I heard, "Uhh uhh, y'all can't hide here! He ain't gonna shoot up my house!"

I looked around to see where the voice was coming from, and spotted the mail slot in the front door pushed open. It was the same neighbor I caught spying on me earlier, now peeking and talking through the slot.

"My moms is shot lady! Why you gonna do us like that?!"

"I'm sorry, but y'all gotta move from here.

I don't want or need none of this drama," she replied.

Milford began to slowly walk in our direction. He was walking in and out of the neighboring yards, and looking all around the parked cars for us. Then he started shouting,

"Don't hide now nigga! I thought you was hard! You think you can cut me on my face, then slide? I'm a kill you and your hoe ass momma!"

I was busy trying to convince this lady to let us stay where we were, meanwhile he was closing in on us. And now we were in his line of sight. There was no where to run or hide. Suddenly the lady stopped talking and the mail slot closed. I slowly turned my head, and Milford and I, locked eyes. For a split second there was dead silence… Then I heard,

"Police! Drop the gun! Drop the gun! Don't make me say it again! I will shoot you right where you stand!"

Milford had his arm fully extended with his pistol pointed at my head. He started to mumble something, but I couldn't make it out. I won't even front, I was scared as shit. I thought this was the end. But surprisingly, fat boy put the gun down. This so-called cop ran up, put cuffs on him, and made him sit down on the curb. I say so-called cop, cause this guy was dressed in pajama pants and had slippers on. He looked crazy. And he never showed a badge. Evidently, he was driving past, saw what was going on, and decided to stop. Lucky for me!

As for my moms, she wasn't looking good at all; I could still see her breathing, besides that, she was motionless. I cradled her head in my lap, while we lingered behind the bushes. I tried to see where she was shot, but couldn't find any wounds. There was no blood, no holes in her clothes, nothing. I began to shake her head and call out her name to try and wake her. The neighbor who just told me to get out her yard, came out of the house holding a wet rag and some other medical stuff. Now she wanna act like she's nurse Betty or some shit. I was about to curse her ass out, but changed my mind when my mom started to come to. It turned out that she wasn't shot. She only fainted. Thank God she's ok.

In the background you could hear the sirens of the different emergency vehicles coming closer. I whispered in my mom's ear that I had to bounce, and that I'd be back. I couldn't wait around for the Po-Po. I had to leave her in the care of her fucked up neighbor. I figured it would only have to be for a few minutes, cause the Calvary was on their way.

Pajama cop had his gun aimed at Milford's face, and his cell phone tucked between his shoulder and his jaw. He was yapping away. It was like he forgot I was even there. That was the perfect opportunity to slip away, but as soon as that nigga Milford saw me trying to break out, he started yelling,

"So you just gonna let him go?!"

He motioned his head in my direction, making Pajama cop turn around and put his sights on me.

"Buddy stay put. Wait till my backup gets here, and we'll sort this all out," he said.

At first I stopped, but as he continued to talk, I inched further and further away from him. He kept pointing his gun back and forth between Milford and I. And telling us both to stay put. Milford kept trying to stand his fat ass up, and he kept pushing him back down. He told me to keep my hands on the hood of his car, and not to move.

The sirens got louder and the first of three cop cars turned the corner, followed by an ambulance. As they approached, I could see the relief on Pajama cop's face, he became more relaxed. That was my opening. I saw a chance to run. I took a deep breath and hauled ass through the neighbor's yard. In anticipation of getting shot, I flexed my back muscles to try and cushion the impact of the bullets. I cleared the backyard fence, and made it out to the main street. He never chased after me or fired his gun. I was home free.

Trust & Believe

147

11 "THE TRUST OF THE INNOCENT IS THE LIAR'S MOST USEFUL TOOL." - STEPHEN KING

"**D**id y'all arrest him yet?"

That was the first question Tiffany asked before she sat down with the detectives at the Police station.

"No ma'am we haven't," one officer said, "but don't worry we're working on it."

"What's the delay? Y'all can't find him? Why did y'all ask me to come back down here?" she asked.

"We need your help to clear up a few more things."

"Clear up what? I thought I told you guys everything. I gave you the names of his friends, where he hangs out at, everything."

"Yes we know ma'am and it was real helpful; but we need a little more. What can you tell us about his mom?"

"Who? Charlene? I mean what exactly do y'all want to know?… She really doesn't have anything to do with this."

"It's nothing serious. We just need to know a little bit about her background, and any dealings you may have had with her in the past."

"Well, I can't tell y'all much. All I can say is that we used to be close. She was like my sister. It's not like that anymore though. I don't know what's going on with her these days."

"Is it because of Robert?"

"Naw, It was getting shaky way before that."

"How so?"

"I dunno, it's hard to explain, I mean... We just stopped hanging out like we use to. She was always stressing about something, and that made her hard to be around."

"Well we went by her house looking for Robert the other day, and it looked like someone gave it to her good."

The confused look that Tiffany displayed, made the officer reveal a little more.

"Somebody beat her up bad. We're talking black eyes, busted lips, the whole nine. We ended up having to return shortly thereafter to investigate a totally different situation. We're thinking that Robert may have had some involvement in that situation."

"Wow, that's interesting... But I'm saying like, why would y'all go by her house looking for him, when I told y'all before that he wouldn't be there? He has mad problems with her boyfriend."

"That's the only address we had on record, so we had to follow up. He was supposedly released to his mom. In fact, she told us that we just missed him. That he had already left for school. Now, is there something we're missing? Something that you're not telling us?"

Her eyes darted back and forth from one officer to the other as she shook her head no.

"So, you don't think Robert would hurt his mother?"

"Eh, eh, no he wouldn't do that to his momma."

"How can you be so sure? Look what he did to you."

"It's different. I ain't his momma. Robert loves Charlene to death. He'd go all out for her. He'd never hurt her."

"We already have her boyfriend in

custody, but he's not copping to it."

"Who? Milford?"

"Yeah. Do you think he's capable of doing something like that?"

"No, he wouldn't touch her. At least I don't think he would. They used to argue a lot about Robert, but other than that, they were cool. Plus Charlene wouldn't go for that, especially not from him."

"Why would you say that?"

"She got him in check. If you ask me, I think he's a little scared of her. She talks to him any old kinda way, disrespects him in public and everything. She doesn't care who's around; and he never says nothing back."

"Well if not him, who? Somebody had to do it. She wouldn't do that to herself."

"Why didn't y'all ask her? I'm saying like, y'all questioning me like I know."

"We did, but she's not talking. That's why we're asking you. Have you or your girlfriend come into contact with her lately?"

"No! And please leave Kelly out of this. Didn't I just finish telling you guys that me and Charlene don't hang out anymore? What is it that y'all don't understand?"

"We understood you perfectly fine ma'am,

but maybe she didn't like the idea of you filing a report against her son. Did she confront you about it? If she did, and you defended yourself, we totally understand."

"Wait a minute, how did this go from y'all asking for my help, to trying to blame me for some shit that happened to Charlene?... Listen, I didn't have anything to do with that. This was supposed to be about what Robert did to me, but since y'all are trying to turn this all around, I'm ready to drop the whole thing. I don't want to do this anymore. I don't wanna talk. I'm ready to go!... Can I leave now officers? I don't got nothing more to say."

"We'll let you go in a sec, but we're still gonna follow through with the case. You already put the ball in motion; there's no turning back now."

Both detectives got up and left the room, leaving the door slightly ajar, and Tiffany in the line of sight of anyone who passed.

That day just happened to be unusually busy. The precinct was buzzing with activity and jam packed with people.

One of those people, a woman, had stopped or was placed just outside of the door; probably on purpose. She was sporting a dirty pink nylon jacket, and had a red scarf draped over her shoulder. Even though the woman's back was turned to her at the time, Tiffany knew right away who it was, and she quickly tried to cover her face with her hands.

"Tiff, Tiffany, is that you?" the woman asked.

After realizing that she was busted, Tiffany lowered her hands and tried to play it off like she was surprised.

"Hey Charlene. What's up girl, what are you doing down here?"

"I should be asking you the same thing," Charlene replied.

"Oh my God Charlene, what happened to your face? Is that why you're here? I was just about to leave. They brought me down here to question me about some random bullshit."

"Bullshit about what?"

"Some bullshit about Robert that I absolutely know nothing at all about, but don't worry I didn't tell them anything."

"There's nothing for you to tell. That's kinda funny though; why would they wanna talk to you just out of the blue?"

"I don't know. They probably found out

that I'm his Godmother and figured I knew what was going on with him. You know what I'm saying? Who knows?"

Charlene smirked, sucked her teeth, then exploded.

"So out of all the people they could've talked to, they chose you. You're the one that knows everything that's going on in MY son's life. Uh huh, I see… Bitch I know why your down here! You need to stop your lying! I should drag your stanking ass all over this precinct. You're trying to get my son locked the fuck back up, all because he doesn't wanna fuck with you no more! You're a pedophile! A motherfucking pedophile! He told me everything!"

Tiffany leaned back in her chair, apparently shocked by the sudden outburst. Before she had a chance to gather herself, Charlene pounced on her. She had entered the room, and charged across the table.

An officer that was passing by, saw what was going on, grabbed Charlene from behind and held her.

The detectives quickly hustled back into the room and got between the ladies while they screamed and cursed at each other.

One detective pulled Charlene out of the

room and took her down the hallway; while the other stayed behind with Tiffany.

Once everything simmered down, he asked,

"Are you sure you don't have nothing else to say?"

"That's fucked up what y'all did! Y'all put her outside the room on purpose and left the door open. I came to you guys for help and look what y'all did to me?" Tiffany replied.

"What did we do? We were only trying to help you."

"I should've never done this. I should've never came down here. What the hell am I gonna do now?"

Trust & Believe

12 "LIFE ISN'T ABOUT FINDING YOURSELF, LIFE IS ABOUT CREATING YOURSELF." - GEORGE BERNARD SHAW

When I showed up at Tap's door, I was hot. Not so much because he left me, but literally hot from walking the four miles to get to his house. I was not only hot, I was tired, and sweaty.

I could see him grinning through the window before he even opened the door; and I couldn't wait to hear his stupid ass explanation.

"Hey bro where you been? I was looking for you," he said.

Even though I was aggravated I hid it behind my smile, and responded to him in a mellow tone of voice.

"Yo, why did you bolt on me B?"

The silly little smirk on his face disappeared, and he started to stutter and stumble over his words.

"Umm, umm, bullets don't have no names bro, and besides, you ran too."

"I didn't run. I was just walking fast. Unlike you, who jumped in the car and dipped!"

"I only drove around the block bro. By the time I came back, there were cops all over the place. I didn't see you or your mom anywhere, so I kept going."

"Yo, you got mad excuses B. It doesn't take 20 minutes to drive around the corner. And you mean to tell me that you didn't see my moms laid out there on the ground?"

"Umm, Nah, I didn't see her. What happened, is she ok?"

"She's alright; at first I thought she got shot, but she only fainted. I figured the cops or somebody, would've taken her to the hospital to get checked out, but when I went up there, they said they had no record of her. And it keeps going to voicemail every time I try to call her. By chance, did she call over here looking for me?"

"Nope, she didn't call here."

"Dam, where the hell is she?"

I wasn't actually asking him the question, I was whispering it to myself out of frustration.

I stood there silent for a few seconds before I asked to use his phone. He quickly opened the storm door and moved to the side so I could pass. The phone was in an area right off his living room. It was an antique styled phone in which you put one part to your ear, and speak through the other. Some old Andy Griffith type shit.

I placed the call, and ironically my mom picked up right away.

"Hello, ma?"

"Robert? is that you?"

"Yeah ma it's me. Where are you? I've been trying to reach you all day. What hospital are you in?"

"I'm not in the hospital Robert, I'm at the precinct."

"The precinct?"

"Uh huh, I never went to the hospital. I didn't feel like I needed to go, so they brought me directly here."

"For what?"

"What do you think Robert?... After all that went on, you're gonna ask me some dumb shit like that? Really Robert?... They brought me here to be questioned, but I'm fin to walk out right now. There's a lot I got to tell you; but I don't wanna do it over the phone."

"Ok ma, okay, you don't have to jump down my throat. But real quick, what's up with Milford?"

"Ha, that nigga's ass is done. We won't have to worry about him for a while. He's probably gonna go and cry to his momma for help, but she ain't gonna bail him out. That bitch ain't got no money, and she's definitely not putting up her house. What's that I hear in the background? Where are you? Are you calling me from that boy's house?"

"What boy?"

"Come on Robert, don't play stupid. You know exactly who I'm talking about."

"Yeah ma, okay, I'm with him. He's in another room watching tv. That's probably what you hear."

"Robert listen to me, you need to dead that friendship. Get up out of that boy's house, stop asking him for favors, he's not who you think he is. He's no good."

"I don't know why all of a sudden you have a problem with him ma; but are you gonna come pick me up?"

"In what Robert? Milford fucked up my

car. You're gonna have to walk. I don't think you should take a chance on the train. They're probably looking for you."

"Who?"

"The cops Robert, the cops!"

"For what? What did they say ma? Is it because of Milford?"

"No, it's not for that; It's for that shit that happened between you and Tiffany!"

"I thought you talked to her. You said it wasn't gonna be a problem; that she wasn't gonna squeal."

"I did talk to her, but shit changed. Just come Robert, we'll talk about it later. Meet me down at the Chinese restaurant that we always go to as soon as you can."

"All right I'm on my way, but dam ma it seems like everything is worse now than it was before."

"I know Robert I know, but we can't solve shit over the phone. So come on now you're wasting time."

"Wait ma don't hang up!"

I couldn't let the conversation end without telling her one last thing, and I purposely lowered my voice so Taps wouldn't over hear it.

"I heard what you said earlier about Taps,

but I still feel like I owe this nigga for bailing me out. I just can't cut him off, It's not that simple."

"Fuck him Robert. Fuck him and his bail money! Everything will work itself out. Trust and believe. Now bring your ass on! And stay off of the main streets."

I hung up the phone and quickly walked toward the living room. Taps was in there sitting on the couch with his feet propped up on the coffee table. He had one hand holding the remote, and the other tucked down in his pants. If I didn't know any better, it looked like he was scratching his nuts. I stuck my head in and yelled,

"Yo thanks B. I'll see you later I gotta bounce."

"Everything okay bro? You need a ride?"

"Nah B I'm good. Everything is cool."

"Oh shit! Robert Wait a minute, Come here! Quick!"

He waved me into the room. I stepped in, looked up at the tv, and my jaw dropped.

Plastered across the screen was the face of that hoe we picked up the other night.

The news anchor started the report by saying that a guy who was walking his dog, found her body on the side of the road. The police were asking anyone who had any information to call the tip line. The crime stoppers were offering a one thousand dollar reward.

When the reporter at the scene began to interview her family, the family got real emotional. They immediately started crying, and falling all out in the street.

The man who was supposedly her boyfriend, jumped in front of the camera and started yelling that he wanted justice. He didn't have a tooth in his mouth, but wanted to do all the talking. On top of that, his english was horrible. Neither I, Taps, or the reporter giving the interview, could understand anything this motherfucker was saying. He did look mad familiar though.

By the time they finished the story, I was feeling sick to my stomach.

Taps on the other hand, had a big gigantic smile on his face.

"Can you believe that bro? It made the news! I can't believe it!" He yelled.

"Shhh shhh, keep it down B."

"Don't worry bro, my parents ain't here. Shit I can't believe it. We're famous!"

"What the fuck you mean we're famous? YOU'RE FAMOUS MOTHERFUCKER,

NOT ME! I don't wanna have nothing to do with it! You're the one that hit that bitch over the head. If they find out, do you know how much time you're looking at? Don't drag me into your shit!"

"Don't worry bro, you don't have to be scared."

"Yo you're bugging B, I ain't scared of nothing! You can chill out with all that. I'm just not trying to get 25 to life over this bullshit."

"Calm down dude, nobody's going to jail. Everything will be cool."

"I hope so B… but yo, I gotta get out of here and meet up with my moms. Can we put this to bed? Or do I have to worry about you running your fucking mouth to everybody?"

"My lips are sealed."

He put his index finger and thumb together, and ran them across his lips; demonstrating how he was zipping them closed.

But as he followed me to the door, he yet again blurted out,

"I can't believe it bro, It made the fucking news!"

It was like he didn't hear a dam thing I

said, and that made me paranoid.

After I left his house, I was constantly looking over my shoulder and jumping every time I heard a siren. I was expecting the five-o to swoop in and scoop me up at any given moment.

I did take my mom's advice though, and stayed my ass off of the main streets, but it made the trip that much longer.

From where Tap's house is located to the Chinese restaurant is hella far, even when you take the major road. I was trying to get there on the back streets.

There was no way in hell I was gonna make it in a reasonable amount of time; and I didn't want to make my moms wait.

So when this opportunity came my way, I didn't hesitate, I took it.

There was some little kid out riding his bike. He was riding back and forth, up and down the sidewalk. I walked towards him, put on a friendly harmless smile, and immediately jacked him for his bike.

If the circumstances were different, I probably wouldn't have done it, but at that moment I felt I had to. It was just starting to get dark, he shouldn't have been outside by himself anyway, and where was his momma at?

I give little man props for trying to fight back, nevertheless, I still ended up rolling off with his bike.

A couple of Puerto Rican cats that were chilling inside a corner store, saw what was going on and ran out to try and stop it. They chased me for about a block or two, but eventually gave up and I got away.

Not too long after, I rolled up in front of the Chinese restaurant. My mom was already there, arguing like usual, with who I thought, was one of the Chinese people who worked there. She's always arguing with them about the price or how they prepare her food, so I didn't think nothing of it.

I hopped off the bike and walked in. That's when I realized it wasn't the restaurant worker she was arguing with, it was some random young chick.

I startled them both when I came through the door, but the young girl turned around first. To my surprise it was Keke.

A chair was positioned between the two of them, and Keke was holding on to the back of it. As soon as she saw me she yelled out,

"Robert you better get your crazy ass

momma from out of my face, before I buss her over the head with this chair!"

I didn't have a chance to make a move, because a bunch of Chinese people came out of nowhere and surrounded me. The guy who was cooking the food jumped over the counter, and tried to get in between Keke and my mom.

My mom wouldn't back off though. She continued to press Keke hard, and kept pushing the cook out of the way. He managed to grab her by the sleeve of her jacket, and dragged her toward the door of the restaurant.

I threw a wild punch that caught him in the back of the head, and he let go of her; but she was immediately tackled to the floor by someone else.

They started hitting us with anything and everything they could get their hands on. Kitchen utensils, shoes, cardboard boxes, you name it.

Before I knew it we were outside on the sidewalk, and Keke was nowhere in sight.

My mom had what looked like duck sauce, all in her hair; and I was laying in a pile of garbage. The Chinese cats had scrambled back inside the restaurant and locked the door.

In the midst of the scuffle somebody rode off with the bike that I just stole. Most likely it was one of the bystanders who had gathered out front to watch the fight.

The only positive thing that came out of this is that the cops weren't called; but we weren't 100 percent sure. We quickly left and headed towards my mom's house. That probably wasn't the best place to go, but at that moment it was the closest.

As we walked along my mom started to explain what had happened.

"I had placed an order and was sitting there waiting for you to come," she said. "Keke walked in. I spoke to her nicely. I didn't plan on treating her any different just because her mother and I aren't seeing eye to eye. I really didn't think she knew anything about the situation between you and Tiffany, but evidently, Tiffany must have told her something, cause she got an attitude with me. I asked her what her problem was, and she said she didn't have a problem. She said it all stank, and that pissed me off. One thing led to another, and I straight up told her; *'don't disrespect me little girl, or I'll slap the shit out of you.'* And that's when you walked in."

"Ma, all of that drama because you didn't like what she said?"

"It wasn't what she said, it's how she said it. But forget her, let me tell you what happened down at the precinct."

Before she could begin, a female's voice loudly chimed in from across the street,

"There they go right there!"

A little beat up red car made a quick u-turn and pulled up along side of us.

Keke was in the passenger seat, and Kelly was driving.

The car stopped, and Kelly got out huffing and puffing; fully dressed in her C.O. uniform. My mom handed me her purse, and put her guard up.

"What you wanna do bitch?" She said.

Kelly backed up.

"This ain't about you Charlene. This is about Robert. He needs to turn himself in."

I began to think about all the mess that I got into over the last couple of days, and really felt like giving up, but my mom wasn't about to let me do that.

"Robert get out of here! Run!" She said.

Kelly reached down into her waistband and pulled out a revolver.

"Don't do it Robert! I already called the cops and they're on their way. Stay put until they get here!"

"You gonna pull a gun out on my son? Are you crazy bitch? You ain't no cop!" my mom said.

"Step away from me Charlene. Don't make me hurt you!"

"So now you're gonna shoot me huh? That's what we doing bitch? Pulling out guns and threatening motherfuckers?"

As my mom moved closer to Kelly, Kelly kept screaming for her to back up.

"Ma chill, I'll just wait here for the cops."

"No Robert get out of here! I'm not gonna let you turn yourself in. She'll have to shoot me first."

"Ma wait! No!"

"She lunged for the gun and grabbed it. They struggled for a brief moment, then KAPOW! It went off, and they both fell to the ground.

I had ducked momentarily after I heard the blast, but sprang back up, and ran over to see if my mom was ok. She was. And Kelly was too. Other than being a little shook up, they were both fine.

Kelly was on her knees patting the

ground, searching for her gun. It had slid under the car and was resting against one of the rear tires. I spotted it before she did, and reached under the car and grabbed it.

The whole time this was happening, Keke never got out of the car. She sat there in the same position, the whole entire time, and didn't move.

I pointed the gun at Kelly, and told her to stand up and move away from the car. Then I banged on the trunk with my fist, and told Keke to get out. She didn't respond.

She didn't turn her head or nothing.

I started to yell,

"Keke get the fuck out the car!"

I knew she heard me, cause the window was down; still nothing.

With the gun aimed at Kelly, I walked along the side of the car, got by the passenger window, and saw Keke's head leaning over to the side. Blood was coming out of her ear.

Suddenly my mom screamed.

"Oh God, Keke's been shot!"

It startled me. I tripped and fell backwards over the curb when I tried to move away.

I ended up dropping the gun, and Kelly

was right there to pick it up.

"Lord have mercy, is she still alive? Is she breathing?" my mom asked.

Kelly opened the car door, checked her pulse, did some other shit, and nodded her head,

"Yeah she's breathing."

My mom picked up her purse from off of the ground, and pulled out her cell phone.

"Let me call an ambulance!"

"Put the phone down, the police are already on their way," Kelly said.

"But we need an ambulance not the police."

"Put the Goddamn phone down Charlene, I ain't gonna tell you no more! If you would've listened from the jump, this shit would've never happened. Now I gotta figure out how to clean this up."

My mom and I stood there for a moment scared to death, trying to figure out what to do next. This was like deja vu to me, the only exception was Keke wasn't dead. But if we didn't do something soon she would be.

"Kelly she needs help right now, we can't wait on the police," my mom said.

"No! We don't need to get anyone else involved. In fact y'all should go. Y'all need to go right now! I'll handle the police when they get here. I'm probably gonna lose my job behind this shit, but y'all being here will just complicate things."

"But you're the one that called them on us. What's gonna happen when they get here, and we're no where around? Are You gonna say that we're responsible for this?"

"I wouldn't do that Charlene."

"Yeah right. I would've never believed that you would pull a gun and call the cops on us either, but you did."

"Okay fuck it then. Stay here and wait for them with me. Y'all will be the ones not going home tonight. They won't give two fucks what you or Robert will say. You both will be automatically guilty."

My mom thought about it for a minute, then grabbed me by my arm, and we bounced. She still continued on with her riffing though, as we high tailed it down the street.

"I know that bitch gonna blame us for that shit, I just know it," she said.

After we got about a block and a half away, another gunshot rang out. We paused for a brief moment, looked at each other, then proceeded on. I guess we both assumed that it wasn't what we thought it was, so we intentionally didn't look back.

13 "OUR DEAD ARE NEVER DEAD TO US, UNTIL WE HAVE FORGOTTEN THEM." - GEORGE ELIOT

I was in total shock when I later found out that Keke didn't make it. The details were sketchy, but deep in my heart I knew that Kelly was responsible. When we left them that evening Keke was still alive. All she needed was some medical attention. I don't know if the ambulance or police ever came. And that gunshot we heard; I still don't know what that was all about, but "Rest In Peace Keke."

It took almost a month for her funeral to happen. Money had to be raised to bury her. I didn't go to the service, but I attended the gathering at the cemetery. I was far enough away not to be noticed, but close enough to see what was going on.

The police had under cover officers

planted all over the place, and they stood out like a sore thumb. What would make them think that a crew of all white cops could possibly blend in with a group of niggas, and not stand out? Everybody there knew who they were, what they were there for, and it still didn't matter; the main suspect was in plain sight.

She played it up good too. With all her hooting and hollering, falling out over the casket after they pulled it out the hearse, and crying her fake tears; this dike was a real actress. She acted more distraught than Keke's own momma. I know people may have looked at her like she was a mother to Keke too; but dam, it was a bit much.

Kelly and Tiffany stood side by side, along with my mom, and completely blocked my view of the casket. Despite all the beef between them, they temporarily put it aside, and came together for the funeral. It was a good look, even though the occasion was sad.

Their outfits were almost identical, down to the stitching on their dresses. They each had on black blouses, dark sunglasses, and wide brimmed hats that they clung on tight to, cause the wind was fierce that day.

It was the first time I ever saw Kelly in a dress. Normally she'd either be in some over sized sweat pants, or her uniform. I won't lie she looked half way decent; almost lady like, but she still had that rough edge to her.

One of the detectives that originally arrested me was in attendance, and it looked like he was communicating with her on the low. Every so often she would glance over at him, and he'd slightly nod his head. Whatever they were doing, I wasn't on his radar; and I wanted it to stay that way.

Kelly knew I was there, and where I was posted up at. She could have easily sent them my way. She also knew that I've been chilling at my mom's crib since all this shit happened, and not a single officer came by to look for me. I'm not a snitch, but in this case I swear to God if either me or my mom would've went down for Keke's murder, Kelly would've went down with us; and I think she knew that. So at that moment, as far as I was concerned, we were good.

I still kept a low profile though. I mostly came out at night, and I limited my interaction with my friends.

One thing that wouldn't go away, was the incident that happened between me, Taps, and that hoe we met outside the Port Authority. The news had covered it at least three times, and the police were now asking the community for help.

The reward crept up to $10,000. For some people that's not a lot of money, but for broke niggas like me in the hood, that's dam near a million dollars. So I got nervous every time the story broadcasted.

My mind would start to wander; thinking that Taps would be out some where running his mouth, bragging, and be over heard by someone who would call the tip line seeking the reward. No matter how hard I tried, I just couldn't trust that he would keep his mouth shut.

When I would watch the news at night for new developments in Keke's case, that hoe's report would pop up. You would think that after a week or so they would quit running it; but they didn't.

My mom never really paid attention to it, but on this particular night she did. They went through the whole dam story like it just happened; from start to finish. When they got to the part where they showed her picture, that's when my mom chimed in.

"I know that bitch," she said. "That's the

bitch Manuel use to mess with! She used to live upstairs from us, remember Robert?"

I knew she looked kinda familiar. I was young at the time, but once she pointed it out, it all started to come back.

I even remembered who that toothless guy was that was all up in the camera. It was none other than Manuel.

"Oh my God, look how bad he looks Robert. I did the right thing by getting rid of his ass! I dodged a bullet!"

My mom continued to ramble on, and I didn't say a word. She was glued to the tv, and when it was over she came to her own conclusion.

Shaking her head she said, "Umm, umm, umm, it's so sad to hear what happened to that girl. Manuel probably got her hooked on drugs, and my guess is she started hoeing to support her habit. I bet you she was murdered by some freaky white boy from the suburbs. He probably killed her, then had sex with her dead body. They're known for doing shit like that. I know first hand, that's why I left your father. He was quick to choke a bitch. Speaking of freaky white boys, your buddy came by the other day, but I didn't answer the door."

That was news to me, because he never came by here before. It was always the other way around; where I would be the one seeking him out.

He's either looking to get his bail money back, or it had to be something to do with that hoe. It's one or the other.

I tried to convey to my mom that it was for the money, but she wasn't trying to hear it. For some reason, that she had yet to explain, did not want me around him.

"Why is he looking for his money already Robert? He can't wait for your trial? Win or lose he'll get his money back. His ass needs to stop stressing. Shit, I thought he had it like that, the way he throws money around like he's some type of big shot."

"Ma, you were only around him one time, how do you know what he does with his money?"

"I know Robert, I know! He might have you fooled, but I know just the type of nigga he is."

It wasn't like I was defending him, but she started to get me pissed off. She refused to tell me what her issues were, but expected me to believe everything she said was fact; with no proof.

"You mad Robert? Don't be mad. I'm just trying to keep you safe that's all. I don't want nothing to happen to my baby. You just don't know how upset I got when I found out that you were locked up. It just killed me. I promised myself once you got out, if I could help it, I wouldn't let you go back. I'd rather you die, then have to spend the rest of your life behind bars like some animal. You'd be in hell everyday. If you're dead, you'll at least be at peace."

"That's some fucked up thing to say ma. If I'm dead you'll never see me again. At least in prison you can visit me."

"I don't wanna visit you in prison Robert. Taking that trip up there, being searched and humiliated, seeing you for a little while, and then having to leave without you, is heart wrenching. To do it over and over again, year after year for however many years, or until you die; it would really take a toll on me. It was hard enough to do it when you were in the Bronx; and that's somewhat close. Imagine if you were up near Canada, or out of state somewhere."

"Dam ma, I'm sorry. I didn't realize that it was such a burden on you. Now I wish you would've never found out."

"I didn't say it was a burden Robert, I'm just trying to explain to you how I felt. It was painful, and I never wanna feel that way again. So listen to me when I tell you I don't want you around that boy. If y'all get caught up doing something you're not supposed to be doing; it could be something minor, you're the one that's gonna go to jail, not him. His funny looking ass will be home, in his room, playing Nintendo and jerking off."

We stared at each other for a minute or so, then burst out laughing. I guess we both imagined what that picture would look like, and it tickled us. But the laughter quickly turned to tears. It had been an emotional couple of months.

I really wanted to tell her about the incident with Manuel's girlfriend, but that would've sent her over the edge. It also seemed like she wanted to express something to me, but for reasons that she only knew, was holding back. And there were a couple of other issues that were mounting. Like the problems I had with Tiffany. They really weren't squashed, even though her and my mom were now cordial; and this whole thing with Keke wasn't even close to being resolved.

After leaving the cemetery, everyone was supposed to meet back at Tiffany's apartment for the reception, and my mom wanted me to come. She told me that it's only right that I pay my respects, cause at the end of the day, we were like family. She wanted me to put all my beefs aside, and come together for Keke's sake.

What she was saying was cool, but I was still skeptical about going. Not because I haven't seen or worked out the issues I had with Tiffany, but I didn't wanna run into any cops who might be there.

I met my mom outside the building. She had already been inside, scoped out the place, and asked Tiffany if it was okay for me to come up. She said it was. I was still apprehensive about it, but returned to the reception with my mom.

Tiffany's apartment was hot as hell, smelled like roach spray, and was packed to the brim with guests. There were Keke's classmates who came with their parents, some people who knew her from the building, and a few of Tiffany's friends, who brought a friend, plus one. No matter the occasion, good or bad, niggas ain't gonna miss out on a meal.

Kelly was bouncing off the walls. She was sweating profusely, hugging and kissing people on their cheeks, and she wouldn't shut the fuck up. I thought she was high, because she was acting way out of character.

My mom and I had separated at the door. She went off to mingle with some people she knew, and I walked straight over to Kelly.

Thinking we were cool, I extended my hand out to greet her. She looked me dead in my face, sucked her teeth, and turned away. I was about to flip, but people were looking, and I didn't wanna cause a scene. I played it off like I was trying to go around her to shake someone else's hand, and reached out to an old man who was standing behind her. It worked. The old man was so excited that I was shaking his hand, that he wouldn't let it go. I stood there chatting, and holding his clammy hand, for almost 20 minutes. I had to make the excuse of having to use the bathroom, in order for him to let go.

As soon as our conversation ended, and I turned to walk away, out of nowhere came Tiffany. She stepped right in front of me

with her arms wide open, looking for a hug.
I was hesitant at first, but after we embraced
I felt at ease.

"I'm glad you came Robert, I really am.
Keke would've wanted this. I'm so sorry,"
she whispered.

"I'm sorry too Tiff. For everything."

She began to weep uncontrollably. I sat
her down on the couch, knelt in front of her,
held and rubbed her hand to try and
comfort her.

Kelly rushed over to see if she was alright.
The dirty look she gave me, made it seem
like I was the cause of Tiffany's sudden
outburst. Like it absolutely had nothing to
do with her just burying her daughter.

Tiffany assured her she was ok, but Kelly
would not let her be. She'd come by every
couple of minutes and interrupt us.

"Are you sure you're alright? Do you
want to lay down? Maybe you need some
time alone."

It was obvious that she didn't want me to
talk to her. She probably didn't want me
there at all.

To spite her, I decided to whisper in
Tiffany's ear on purpose. It was only
gibberish, but I wanted to make Kelly think

that I was talking about her. I made sure to look dead in her face every time I did it, and I know it annoyed her.

The little voice inside of me said,

"Nah bitch I ain't talking about you, but if you keep fucking with me I just might let the cat out the bag."

And there was a lot I could've said. I didn't know all the details, but if I were to put some of the pieces together it wouldn't look good for Kelly at all.

When we left the area that night, Keke was unconscious but still alive. About 2 minutes after we left we heard a gunshot. The next day we find out that Keke was dead. She was reportedly shot twice.

The gun only went off once when Kelly and my mom were struggling. Who shot her the second time? It had to be Kelly. There was no one else around. The only thing I couldn't figure out was why.

The mood of the reception became a little more upbeat, when someone turned on the music. Then one of Tiffany's neighbors, who had one too many drinks, decided he'd say a few words. Slurring heavily he began to speak,

"She was a beautiful little girl. I remember

when she was in diapers. She loved to jump rope, and she loved to read. Every time I'd see her she'd have a book in her hand. We're gonna miss you Keke, we're really gonna miss you, but I know you're in a better place."

The song **'Just Us'** came on by **Two Tons of Fun**, and people started to move and bob their heads a little. Midway through the song, the living room turned into a full blown dance floor.

One of the guests pulled Tiffany up out of her seat to dance. I sat there and watched them for a little while, but later got up and started milling around the apartment.

I ended up in Keke's room. You could tell that no one had been in there since her passing. It was just as she had left it; messy. Clothes were all over the floor, the bed was not made, and magazines were scattered everywhere.

I sat on the edge of the bed, and looked up at all the pictures and awards she had tacked on her wall. Dam, this shit was sad, and I was feeling guilty as hell.

I laid back, put my feet up, and completely stretched out on her bed. Her pillow felt kinda uncomfortable, like there was something hard under it. I lifted it up and found a small notebook, that had flowers and hearts drawn on the cover. The contents of the book were filled with months or it could've been years of her writings. It wasn't written in everyday, she would skip weeks, sometimes months, but it was all dated; and she wrote a lot.

I started to read some of it, and was surprised to find out that she had a big crush on me.

She also wrote a lot about her dreams. How she wished she could've spent more time with her dad; who'd been locked up for over a decade, and how she wished she could have had a normal family life. She wasn't feeling that two momma thing that Tiffany and Kelly were pushing, and she deeply despised them for it.

As I skimmed through, I came to a section where she wrote about Kelly, and it totally caught me off guard.

She wrote that Kelly was trying to turn her out. It started with her making comments about her body, and slowly grew into something else. She explained how Kelly would sneak into her room at night, climb in her bed, and go down on her.

Leaving money on her nightstand, was her way of bribing her not to tell. But that soon progressed into threats.

I kept scrolling through the pages to one of Keke's last entries; where she wrote how she drummed up the nerve to confront Kelly. She told her that she wasn't scared of her anymore, and if she didn't stop touching her, that she was gonna tell her mom.

She never got the chance to.

The more I read the more I got heated.

Suddenly there was a rapid knock on the door. I quickly hid the book under the covers just as the door flew open. It was only my mom. She walked in holding a champagne glass in one hand, and a bottle of liquor in the other.

"Robert, what are you doing in here?" She asked.

I didn't say a word, but the look I had on my face must have said it all.

"What's wrong? What happened?"

"Nothing ma. I'm fin to go."

I got up off the bed, tucked the notebook under my shirt, and marched out the bedroom. I made a bee line straight for Kelly.

She was sitting on the window sill in the

living room, sipping a beer straight out the can. She watched as I charged toward her, pushing people out of my way in the process. She didn't even flinch, she kept on sipping. I balled up my fist, and zeroed in on her jaw. I was planning on bussing her right in her shit, but before I could, I was tackled to the floor.

"Relax buddy relax!"

I was face down with one arm free, and the other pinned behind my back. Some big black dude was on top of me. He had his knee pressed into my thigh, while he struggled to get control of my free arm. When he did, the cuffs came out. That's when I realized he was a cop.

He probably figured that I'd never suspect him, and I didn't. He blended in well. He had on a tacky suit, like all the other older cats that were there, plus he was out of shape, and he didn't interupt the flow of the many blunts that were being passed around the apartment. Shit, he might have even partook in it.

My mom couldn't tell the difference either. She thought he was just some random nigga I was scrapping with, and didn't think twice about going upside his head with the liquor bottle.

Clunk!

The guy fell in slow motion and landed right beside me; he was out cold, and glass was everywhere. My mom stood over him with a remnant of the broken bottle still in her hand. She was nervous and shaking.

"Oh shit he's a cop? Why didn't somebody tell me? Oh God I'm going to jail!"

"Ma calm down! You ain't going no where. Don't worry, just look in his pockets, find the key, and un-cuff me."

The key was inside his suit jacket, and once the cuffs were removed, we bounced.

14 "WHEN SOMEBODY CHALLENGES YOU, FIGHT BACK. BE BRUTAL, BE TOUGH" - DONALD TRUMP

I tossed and turned all night.

When I was finally able to fall asleep, it was no more than an hour that had passed before I was rudely awakened again by my mom.

"Who the fuck keeps ringing the dam doorbell?" she screamed.

That, and the sound of her slippers whisking pass my bedroom door and sliding down the hall, quickly snapped me out of my dreams.

It was around one o'clock in the afternoon. We weren't expecting any visitors, but who ever it was, constantly rang the bell like a fucking retard. It must be Jehovah's Witnesses, or some kids playing around; at least that's what I thought.

It was way too late for it to be the police. I say that because those guys like to come at the crack of dawn and catch a nigga sleeping; plus they hardly ever ring the bell. They'll usually bang on the door real hard with their billy club, or just kick it in.

Since I knew it couldn't possibly be them, I rolled over and went back to sleep.

We both were still exhausted from the day before, and my mom should have done what I did; ignored the door, and stayed in bed. Instead, she decided to answer it.

I was half awake and could only hear rumbles of the conversation. The tone of it started out low, but then the level rose sharply. It rose to the point that I had to get out of bed to see what was going on. When I opened the door to my bedroom, their voices came in loud and clear, and I instantly knew who my mom was arguing with.

It was Taps.

His tenor toned nasally sounding voice, along with my mom screaming a high pitched soprano, echoed through the house like an opera.

I had no idea at all why they would be arguing; other than my mom not really liking Taps too much. But I wouldn't think that alone, would cause all this drama. It seemed personal.

In a short time, I got to know Taps pretty well, and knew he liked to get under people's skin by saying slick shit. But I would've never believed that he would be that disrespectful toward my mom, until I heard it with my own ears.

"I told you before, Robert ain't here! He doesn't live here, his shit ain't here, he doesn't come by here to visit or nothing! So don't bring your ass around here again!" My mom yelled.

I could see Taps finger sticking through the open door and pointing at the couch,

"Why are you lying to me Charlene? His jacket is right there!"

"Charlene? Who do you think you're talking to? Don't you ever call me by my first name little boy, you don't know me like that. It's Miss Riley to you!"

"Well Charlene, I know you gotta birth mark on your ass, and stretch marks on your stomach, not to mention saggy titties. So I would~say that I know you pretty well," he replied.

I was stunned. My body began to tremble

a little, and I could feel the anger building up inside.

I couldn't let him get away with such blatant disrespect. Friend or no friend, I immediately confronted him.

I slid passed my mom, pushed the screen door wide open, and got right up in his face.

He started hemming and hawing and mumbling something; but I wasn't trying to hear it. I straight punched him right in his face.

The impact knocked him off the steps and into the muddy front yard. I dove on top of him, and we started rolling around in the dirt. Somehow he managed to reverse his position and wound up on top. He then started landing a few blows of his own. I tried my best to get back on top, but all the energy I was exerting made me tired, and he slowly began to get the best of me. I could hear my mom's screams in the background,

"Come on Robert, don't let him do that to you, fuck him up!"

He started to choke the shit out of me; to the point where it felt like I was about to lose consciousness. I couldn't believe that this skinny white boy was kicking my ass in my own yard, in front of my momma. Then to add insult to injury he started talking shit.

"After I finish kicking your ass I'm gonna take your ma inside and have her suck me off again! I know how much she loves white boys!" He shouted.

He had the side of my face pinned to the ground with the palm of his hand, forcing me to stare directly at my mom as he was saying it.

Her whole expression changed.

A look of shock and guilt ravished her face.

She immediately picked up an old brick that was laying around in the yard, and clocked him over the head with it. He slowly rolled off onto his side.

She hit him hard, and by the way he fell over I thought he was dead, but I could see him breathing.

While he laid there holding his head, I got up and kicked him a few times for good measure.

My mom pulled me back.

"Stop Robert he had enough," she said.

Even though I was breathing mad hard, and had blood trickling out my nose, I was still hyped up, and ready to go some more.

Taps staggered to his feet and stumbled

around with his hand palming the side of his head. Once he got his balance he continued to talk shit.

"You fucking niggers better pay me my money back now or…"

"Or what mother fucker? You gonna go to the Police? Go ahead, you ain't the only one that got shit to tell them," I said.

Then my mom interjected,

"Oh, so now we niggers now right?"

I stuck my hand out in front of her trying to let her know that I had it under control, but she wouldn't let up.

"No Robert, this white cracker ass cracker calling us niggers to our face, right in front of our own house, who the fuck he think he is!" She yelled.

I found it funny how she skipped over the part where he said he was gonna have her suck him off again, and focused on the nigger shit. What did he mean by again? And how does he know about your birth mark? Those were the questions I wanted to ask, but couldn't, because right then I had to deal with the situation at hand.

Taps backed his way out of our yard and over to his car, or should I say his grandfather's car, and continued to mouth off.

"Your gonna get yours! You better watch your back, both of you! I got friends, you wait and see!"

"Yeah whatever nigga," I said, as I threw my middle finger up at him.

He jumped in the car and pulled off real fast; leaving behind a cloud of blue smoke, and the smell of burnt oil.

My mom tried to wipe the blood from my nose with the bottom of her robe. I quickly pushed her hand away.

She had some explaining to do.

"No ma I can wipe my own nose."

"What's the matter? What are you upset with me for Robert? I'm just trying to help you."

"What did he mean by that ma?"

"What?"

"Come on ma don't play stupid? Him saying he'll have you suck him off again. And how does he know how your body look? Your birth mark your stretch marks, all that shit!"

"I don't know Robert, I really don't. He was just saying that to get you upset!"

"So you're gonna look me dead in my face and lie to me ma?"

Usually she has so much to say. This time she was quiet. She shook her head, turned around, and walked back inside the house.

I followed her inside, threw on some clothes, and broke out. I didn't tell her where I was going or when or if I'd be back. I needed time to think.

Even though she wouldn't admit it, I knew her and Taps had some kind of encounter and it wasn't good. I thought back to one of the conversations we had while I was locked up, when she said that she'd strip to get the money to bail me out. I really didn't believe it, but if she wasn't joking, how far would she go? I got pissed off just thinking about it. And knowing how Taps was; fuck it, that nigga had to go!

I hopped on the subway and just rode. I got on the A train at the Mott avenue station in Far rockaway, and rode it back and forth to Manhattan until the wee hours of the night. The whole time I was trying to figure out a way to deal with Taps, without having it come back to me.

It was around 2:00am in the morning, and the train was dam near empty. It was just me and some homeless guy, who had the whole car smelling like piss. We were starting to head back downtown from 207th street, and was pulling up into the Dyckman street station in upper Manhattan, Washington Heights to be exact, where all the fly Dominican bitches live. A crowd a people piled onto the train at that stop, and kinda broke my concentration.

It was a bunch of Spanish girls along with a couple of guys, who I figured were all Dominican. I tried not to stare at them, because the clothes the girls had on were tight and revealing, and I know how those Dominican dudes get down, especially when it comes to their women. Even if none of them were their girls, it would be an issue, and I didn't want to get stabbed that night.

One of the girls though, I couldn't help but eyeball. She had on a skirt that came up to her coochie, and it looked like she didn't have on any panties. The guy she was sitting next to, caught me looking, and said something to me aggressively in Spanish. Here we go again, niggas thinking I'm Spanish because of how I look. When I didn't respond, he kept repeating himself louder and louder. The girls were telling him to chill out, but he wouldn't. I didn't really notice the older guy who was standing next to him in the doorway of the train; until the guy whispered something in his ear, and they both turned around and began to stare at me. I ain't gonna front, I started to get a little nervous.

Suddenly the older guy pointed at me and said, in broken English,

"Poppy, you looka familiar Poppy.~Where I know you from?"

I didn't acknowledge him at all at first. I kept looking down at the floor and acting like I didn't hear him. After he repeated himself a couple of times, I began to recognize his accent, and I looked up.

We made eye contact, and I instantly knew who it was. Shit, I just saw the nigga on t.v., but I wanted to wait and see how he would respond to me.

"Robbie is that you? Oh, my, fucking, God, Robbie! You're all grown up!"

"Hey Manuel," I replied.

I stood up to receive his handshake and hug, even though I was still a little nervous.

After all, I'm partially the reason why he did all that time in jail, and though he doesn't know, I'm partially responsible for what happened to his lady.

In Spanish he explained who I was to his friend, and that calmed him down. Before that he was foaming at the mouth, but his attitude toward me changed instantly. He dam near gave me the girl that I was checking out, gift wrapped. He had her sit on my lap, then he grabbed my hand and put it on her thigh.

It was weird.

Once I found out what he did, it explained everything.

He and Manuel were pimps. They just left a club, and were heading downtown to make some more money on the stroll.

Manuel talked nonstop during the slow long ride downtown. I could barely get a word in. By the time we got to Times Square, his stop, he made sure to let me know, that he had no hard feelings toward me or my mom. In fact, he admitted that it was his fault. That he was stupid, and should have never given my mom the combination to the safe.

He asked how she was doing, and I could tell by the look on his face that he still had a little something something for her.

I changed the subject and started talking about how I saw him on the news. I told him that I was sorry for what happened to his lady, and then hinted that I kinda heard something about it. He was all ears. Not so much because he loved and cared about this woman, but because she was his top earning hoe.

Bingo!… This is it, this was how I would solve my problem.

In a round about way, without incriminating myself, I told him that I may know the guy who had something to do with it.

I told him about Taps. Yes I did. I told him where he lived, what he looked like, about his parents, everything. The more I talked the more Manuel's eyes got bigger. I could tell he wasn't going to go to the cops with the info, he was gonna handle this himself, and probably bring his non-English speaking friend along with him. That guy looked like a straight up killer, and Manuel was translating every word I said to him.

Trust & Believe

15 "IT'S SAD WHEN SOMEONE YOU KNOW BECOMES SOMEONE YOU KNEW." - HENRY ROLLINS

Even though a week had already passed since our awkward unplanned reunion, the conversation that I had with Manuel was still weighing heavy on my mind. I hadn't heard anything in the streets, and wondered when or if he and his homey were gonna move on Taps. I hoped something would've happened soon, so things could kinda go back to normal between me and my moms. We were still on the outs. We barely spoke, and tried hard to stay out of each other's way. It was weird, because we never acted like that toward each other before. I was use to her shading Milford and her other friends, but not me. Not her baby boy! Especially not after all the crap we've been through!

That whole Taps situation had my stomach twisted in a knot, and she refused to talk about it. It made me mad at first, but the anger slowly began to die down. I tried to put myself in her shoes, and ask myself; would I be embarrassed to tell my child if I did something that was kinda suspect? Even if it was to benefit them? That's a tough question. After all, I was the cause of it. If I never insisted on her meeting up with Taps; whatever happened, would have never had happened. So I guess she had the right to throw a little shade.

It was short lived though. Here's why, you see our local news broadcast interrupted one of the daytime court shows we were watching. It was significant at the time, because it was one of the only shows that we'd both sat and watched together. It was a good one that day too. Judge Mathis was about to give his ruling when all of a sudden they cut into the program with:

Breaking news, A New York City Corrections officer was found dead on the side of the road in the Bronx this morning, from an apparent suicide. Officer Kelly Thomas, who was on the job a little over 18 months, body was found in her idling

vehicle, parked on the north bound shoulder of the Bronx River Parkway. She was found slumped over in the driver's seat with an apparent self-inflicted gunshot wound to the head.

My mom and I looked at each other in disbelief, and mouthed the words, "Oh shit," simultaneously.

"What the fuck is going on? First Keke, now Kelly? This is too much. Why the hell would she kill herself," my mom uttered.

"Guilt," I replied.

"Guilt? Guilty of what?"

"Come on ma, think about it. You heard the shots just like I did!"

"I don't believe it! Kelly ain't that cold."

"Well who else could of done it? She was the only one out there! And that's not all she did either. Hold on I'll be right back."

I jumped up off the couch and darted straight to my bedroom, then quickly returned with Keke's notebook in my hand. I placed it in her lap and pointed to the section of the page where I wanted her to begin reading.

"Here, check this out. Start there," I said.

I stepped back to gage her reaction.

I watched a frown appear on her face and

wrinkle her forehead, as her eyes scanned down the page. Her hand began to tremble.

"No, oh no, how could she?"

She covered her mouth with her hand, and looked at me in disbelief.

I nodded my head to confirm that what she was reading was real, and not some bullshit. The look of 'see I told you,' was written all over my face.

"I can't believe that dirty bitch did that to that young girl. Tiffany doesn't even know does she?" My mom asked.

"Nah, I would have told her at the repass, but I had just found the book, and decided to confront Kelly first. When I approached her, homeboy got in the way, and everything went crazy."

My mom looked as if a light bulb had just turned on in her head. She clapped her hands together, then pointed her finger at me and said,

"So that's why that bitch was acting all funny and shit. I thought that was her way of grieving. She knew all along what was up, and played everyone like a fool. I can't believe it. Tiffany trusted her too. But she's also partly to blame. That girl know she ain't no dam lesbian, if she was, she would've never fucked around with your little ass. She just had Kelly there to help her pay her bills; and look what happened."

I really didn't know how to take her last statement. It kinda seemed like my mom was dissing me on the low, and blaming Tiffany for the exact same shit she be doing. I mean, she freeloaded off of Milford for years, and she knew good and well that she didn't love that fat motherfucker.

"Ma, how could Tiff know Kelly would do that to Keke?"

"Well she should've known better than to move a stranger in with her child. She only knew Kelly two weeks before she let her move in."

"You did the same thing ma. Twice. You moved in with Manuel first, then Milford, you drug me along with you, and you only knew them for a few days."

"My situation was different."

"How?"

"I could tell what kind of niggas they were. I knew they weren't no dam child molesters!"

"How'd you know?"

"I just knew alright! Don't question me! Did either of them put their finger in your ass?"

"No!"

"Okay then, I was right!"

I was starting to get tired of my mom coming at me sideways like that. You would've thought that I was Milford with all the shit she'd been saying to me lately. I used to laugh when she use to do it to him, now It wasn't so funny. But we were just getting back on speaking terms and I didn't want to blow it, even though deep down I felt like saying something slick back.

She continued to run off at the mouth.

"You got a lot of nerve to question what I did. You need to worry about yourself, and all the mess you got yourself into! You can't blame that on me! If you were feeling some type away about how you was living, you could've went and stayed with your white daddy! It must not of been that bad!"

"Ma, Calm the fuck down! This ain't about me, this is about Kelly, and what she did. Dam!"

"Well I was just letting you know, so you won't get things misconstrued! You tend to be ungrateful for a lot of shit Robert. Remember if it wasn't for me your ass would be still locked up. I put everything on the line for you!"

"Okay ma, okay. I get it!"

"My pride, my dignity, everything! And for you to question me… boy…"

"Okay I'm sorry ma, I'm sorry! Does that make you feel better?"

"It ain't about being sorry. It's about appreciating shit that people done for you! … Namely me!"

"Alright I appreciate everything you ever done for me… Can we talk about Kelly and Keke now ma?"

She rolled her eyes, leant back on the couch, and shook her head. She was obviously still pissed, but at that point I really didn't care.

"So what now ma?"

She placed her hand under her chin and gave me a stern look. I stared right back at her and shrugged my shoulders.

"What?"

"Mind our business Robert. That's what the hell we should do. Mind our business! They're both gone now. So Telling Tiffany about it wouldn't make a dam bit of difference."

"But…"

"There ain't no buts. It would only make

the situation worse. She don't need to know about it! What you need to do is figure out what you're gonna do, cause you can't stay here."

"Why not?"

"What, you think they just gave up on you? You think this shit is over? You're still hot. They can come barging through this door at any time, and I can't deal with all of that right now. It's too much stress. You need to go."

"You can't deal with all of what? Ain't nobody looking for you ma. Plus everything is squashed between me and Tiff. Who's gonna come barging through the door?"

"Just because you squashed it with Tiff doesn't mean it's squashed with the police. Think Robert think! Use your brain!"

"Alright ma if you want me to leave, I'll leave!"

"It's not so much what I want, it's what you need to do. It's not all good out here for you. Don't get upset, take a minute to think about what I'm saying."

Trust & Believe

16 "ACTION IS THE REAL MEASURE OF INTELLIGENCE." - NAPOLEON HILL

"Give me a hand with this Hymie. Listo? Uno dos tres (*Ready? One two three*)," Manuel whispered.

He and his crime buddy Hymie, pried open a back window in Taps house, and climbed in. Armed with hand guns and one flashlight, they quickly and quietly moved through the first floor of the home trying to locate the bedrooms. Most of the house was dark, except part of a hallway that lead to the basement. Hymie held the flashlight, so he automatically led the way. When they finally figured out how to get upstairs, they unexpectedly ran into their first obstacle.

Taps mom.

As soon as she saw them she stopped dead in her tracks, dropped the full basket of laundry she was carrying, and belted out a loud scream. Without hesitation, Hymie grabbed her by her arm, back handed her across the face, and she instantly fell to the floor.

"Cállate perra! ¿Dónde está el niño? (*Shut up bitch! Where's the boy?!*)," he said.

Manuel knelt down beside her, tilted her head back, and calmly asked in English where Taps was.

Sobbing she answered, "Who are you? What do you want with my son? Does he owe you money? I can pay."

"I just want to talk to the boy, that's all," he replied.

"Run Sammy run! Go hide," she yelled.

Manuel looked up at the flight of stairs, then at Hymie, and shook his head.

"Cuidar de ella (*take care of her*),"

He could barely get to his feet before Hymie bashed her in the face with the butt of his gun; breaking her nose, and knocking her unconscious.

"Dios mío, Hymie, al menos podrías haber esperado hasta que me fuera por el camino. Ahora tengo sangre en mi camisa. (*Goodness Hymie you could of least waited till I moved out the way. Now I got blood on my shirt.*)"

Quietly watching the whole scenario play out through the crack of his partially opened bedroom door, Taps frantically hustled his way out the bedroom window and onto the trellis. He used that to scale up the side of the house and onto the roof. He was in such a hurry that he didn't have a chance to throw on pants, a t-shirt, or anything. Superman underoos and dress socks was all he had on.

They'd caught him slipping that early Sunday morning. The sun wasn't even up yet.

The only reason Manuel and Hymie were delayed getting to him, because they forgot to bring the hand drawn map of the layout of the home. Going off memory, they wasted valuable time going from room to room looking for him.

When they finally did locate his room, they saw the window was left wide open and assumed he climbed out of it. Hymie was prepared to go out after him, and was about to, until a car pulled into the driveway, causing Manuel to cautiously hold him back. They both moved to either side of the window so they couldn't be seen, then peeked out to see who it was.

Taps dad had returned from a Dunkin Donuts run.

He got out of the car, grabbed his box of donuts, and tucked a newspaper under his arm. Hands full, he used his foot to close the car door.

Taps tried but failed to get his attention.

"Dad... Dad up here... wait, wait," he whispered.

By the time his dad got to the front door, Hymie was already on him.

He took his gun and placed it in the small of Tap's dad's back, and had his hand covering his mouth. He had snuck out the side door and crept up on him.

Manuel opened the front door from the inside, and Hymie pushed him in. They led him into the living room and pushed him down to the floor.

Taps listened helplessly to his father's moans as they commenced to beat the shit out of him. His cries echoed up through the chimney right into his ears.

"Tell your son to come down off the roof Amigo," Manuel yelled.

"My son? The roof? What are you talking about?"

Hymie slapped him across the head.

"ohhh lord help me, oh God please," Tap's dad cried.

"God only helps those who help themselves amigo. Tell your boy to come down."

Manuel stepped back and let Hymie go to work on him some more. He threw a flurry of punches to Tap's dad's face and body as he tried desperately to block. Hymie really enjoyed putting the beats on him. He started humming the song "Por Debajo de la Mesa", by Luis Miguel, to the beat of his punches.

Meanwhile, Taps mom had regained consciousness, and stumbled her way over to where they were. She saw what was going on, and attempted to help by jumping on Hymie's back to stop him. He quickly flipped her over his shoulder, and she landed on her head. Manuel began to laugh hysterically.

"Estas personas blancas estan locas Hymie. Demonos prisa y atenlos, para poder tratar con el chico. *(These white people are crazy Hymie. Let's hurry and tie them up so we can deal with the boy.)*"

They tied them back to back using electric cords ripped from the living room lamps.

Hymie took off his shoes and socks, then stuffed the socks in their mouths gagging them. He put his shoes back on, and followed Manuel outside to try and locate Taps.

The sun was trying to push its way through the darkness, dimly illuminating the morning sky. From the ground it wasn't enough light to see him, so Hymie, doing what Taps did, used the trellis to climb up onto the roof to look. Taps was no where in sight.

Speaking slightly above a whisper,

"Llenandolo abajo Hymie, no lo mismo haga arriba alli. *(Bring him down Hymie, don't fuck him up up there,)*" Manuel declared.

"El no esta aqui! *(He's not here!)*"

"Que? *(What?)*"

"El no esta aqui!"

Confused, Manuel began to circle the perimeter of the yard while staring up at the roof line in hopes of spotting Taps. He eventually waved to Hymie to come down, after having no luck. The sun was starting to get brighter and he didn't want Tap's neighbors, even though their homes were a good distance away, to see Hymie walking around on the roof.

"Fuck Hymie, where'd he go?"

Hymie shrugged his shoulders expressing to Manuel that he didn't know, while looking to him for direction.

Meanwhile Taps had slid his way down the chimney and back into the house. After locking the doors, he ran straight to the home security alarm panel and pushed the panic button; which triggered the sirens.

"What the fuck!" Manuel yelled, as he looked around to see where the noise was coming from. Through his peripheral he could see Taps standing in the window covered in soot.

They made eye contact.

Taps stuck his tongue out at him, grabbed his crotch, and flipped him off; which enraged Manuel even more. He ran up to the window and began to yell, "I'm gonna kill you puta!"

Hymie had gotten spooked by the sirens and started to run. He grabbed Manuel by his jacket as he passed him, and pulled him away from the window and down the driveway. Unfortunately though, they weren't able to get away.

By the time they made it to the end of the

driveway, two unmarked cars pulled up alongside the curb and blocked them in.

There were a total of four officers that got out of the vehicles, and they had their weapons drawn. The funny thing was that they didn't look like normal police officers. They were dressed in black, wore Yamikas, and had long beards.

Manuel instantly knew who they were from all the years that he use to work in Crown Heights; which is a heavily Jewish and West Indian neighborhood in Brooklyn.

The so-called officers, were members of the Jewish volunteer police group, known as the Shomrim. Manuel also knew something was fishy about them because they were brandishing firearms, which is illegal in New York.

Hymie on the other hand, had no idea who they were. He immediately placed his gun on the ground, and put his hands in the air. When the group spoke to each other in Yiddish, that freaked Him out even more.

Hymie was relatively new to the U.S., and had never heard a language that sounded like that before. He stood there shaking like a leaf as they yelled out commands.

"Keep your hands where I can see them!

Don't make a move," one of them said.

Speaking in Yiddish, another member of the crew blurted out,

"Kuk in di tokhes holes, mir darfn tsu klap aoyf zeyere kep avek! *(Look at these ass holes, we need to blow their heads off!)*"

After peeking out and making sure that the Shomrim had everything under control, Taps exited his house and slowly strolled down the driveway.

He was now wearing what looked like to be his mother's bathrobe and a pair of her fuzzy slippers.

They were pink.

Soot could still be seen covering his neck and chest through the frilly collar of the robe. He walked straight over to Manuel and got right up in his face. Their noses were damn near touching. Taps tried to stare him down, hoping to intimidate him. But being that close only exposed him to all of Manuel's hardness. The bruises on his face, the scar tissue over his eyes, and his toothless smile. Manuel planted a kiss right smack on the tip of Taps's nose.

Taps went crazy and started wailing on Manuel. Manuel laughed it off.

"You hit like a little girl, puta. Come

closer, so I can give you another kiss," he said.

One of the members of the Shomrim clocked him over the head with his gun, and he fell to the ground. But that didn't stop Manuel from popping shit.

"Fuck you puta! Fake wannabe cop! All of you Maricons!"

Manuel had the Shomrim so distracted that they forgot all about Hymie. They left him standing there by himself, with his hands in the air, while they surrounded Manuel.

"So you wanna rob me and my family huh? I don't know why you picked this house, but I'll bet you'll never step foot on this block again," Taps screamed.

He kicked Manuel in the face, and they all joined in. They kicked and stomped him while he flailed around on the ground trying to block the blows.

Suddenly, out of nowhere a black Crown Vic plowed through the group, and bodies went flying everywhere. A couple of guys got run over, including Manuel. Taps landed on the hood of the car, and rode it as it rocketed up the driveway and crashed into the back of his dad's vehicle. After the impact, he slowly rolled off the hood and onto the ground; where he laid face down, motionless.

The door of the Crown Vic opened and out stepped Hymie. He had jumped into one of the cars that the Shomrim came in and tried to get away. The only problem was, he didn't know how to drive.

Hymie walked over to Taps, shook him with his foot, then pushed him over onto his back. He took a good look at him, and yelled out in his horrible English,

"Iz jis da kid Manuel!"

Manuel was on the ground brimming in pain.

"Estupido you ran over my fucking legs! Forget him, get me out of here, take me to the hospital!"

Before Hymie could respond, he was interrupted by the sound of a loud blast.

Everything got real quiet.

Hymie took a deep breath, and slowly gazed up at the beautiful morning twilight. Blood began to bubble up in his mouth. He gurgled and coughed a little, then rapidly collapsed to the ground; leaving a small puff of smoke behind him. As the smoke slowly dissipated, Taps's mom became visible in the background.

She was standing in the doorway of her home, shotgun in hand, and a crazed look on her face.

She began to inch her way down the driveway.

Manuel watched as she moved closer and closer towards him; stepping over one broken up body after the other. He wasn't able to crawl away or hide. All he could do was lay and wait.

"Hymie, you ok? Are you ok Hymie? Shit Hymie what happened? What happened Hymie? Say something Hymie, say something," Manuel cried.

He then began to recite the Lords prayer in Spanish while Tap's mom stood over him. She stared down into his eyes, put the barrel to his forehead, but didn't immediately pull the trigger. It wasn't until he flipped her off, that she made the decision to clap him.

17 "THE MOST IMPORTANT THING IN COMMUNICATION IS HEARING WHAT ISN'T SAID." - PETER DRUCKER

You can always tell when my mom is on the phone from all the screaming. She's so damn loud. Shit, this time I could even hear the person she was talking to through the handset, so just imagine how loud that person is. You'd think that they were talking through two tin cans connected by a string with all of that yelling.

"Are you telling me that Milford made bail?! What?! His momma down there right now?! Thanks girl for giving me the heads up! Talk to you later! bye!"

She slammed the phone down, picked up her jacket and purse, and headed for the door.

"Robert come here real quick, I wanna tell you something before I go."

I nonchalantly strolled into the living room and begrudgingly answered,

"What ma?"

"You know my home girl Stacey that works down at the court house? Well, she just told me that Milford's momma is down there bailing his ass out. I don't know where the bitch got the money, but some how she scraped it up. Can you believe that shit?"

"What you gonna do?"

"I'm going to get an order of protection. If that nigga think he can get bailed out and show his ass up back here like everything is all good, he's crazy."

"Don't worry about him ma; I got something for him if he does."

"Robert please... You don't need to be getting into any more mess. Let me handle this."

"What's the point of you telling me if you don't want me to do anything?"

"I'm telling you so you won't be surprised if he showed up at our door."

"Man eff him. If he comes around here, I'm laying him down, that's my word!"

"Robert listen, let me go down there and handle this the proper way. A lot been going on, and you need to stay off the radar for a little while. What we need to do is go back to our original plan, and get your ass the fuck up outta here. I think more so now than ever. Spending some time with your father right now would be a good thing."

Here we go again with this bullshit. Part of me wanted to believe what she was saying was for my benefit, the other part felt like she was just trying to get me out of the way. Maybe she wanted to hook back up with him. I know it sounds fucked up, but I couldn't think of any other reason why she would express this now; right when he's about to get bailed out.

I was totally stumped.

"What Robert?... Are you just gonna stand there with your mouth open looking stupid?... You need to think about what I'm saying and figure out what you're gonna do. You can't hide in this house forever. Anyway, let me go handle this, and we'll talk later... Okay?"

"Yeah ma, see you later."

I stood in the doorway and watched as she walked from the house to the car; then waited until she pulled off before I shut the door. I came to the conclusion that everything about my mom was different.

She completely changed. The way she looked at me, the way she walked and talked, her demeanor, all changed. I felt like she didn't have my back anymore, and that I couldn't trust her.

It's hard to believe that after all the crap that fat bastard put her through, she'd actually get back with him. That's some bull. Remember, this was only my assumption; I could be wrong, but at that time it completely changed my mood. I went from being a little annoyed, to out right angry. I needed to get out of the house and get some air.

My plan was to head down to the beach, take a stroll on the boardwalk, clear my mind and reevaluate shit; but I made a quick pit stop along the way.

I stopped by the neighborhood bodega to pick up some gum, and on my way in, I recognized a couple of cats that I went to school with standing out front. I went over to say what's up. We laughed and talked about a bunch of stupid shit for a couple of minutes, before one of them abruptly switched up the conversation.

"Yo what's up with your boy? I saw him being wheeled into my mom's job the other day. Me and my sister was in the lobby waiting for her to get off, and we see this fucking ambulance flying through the parking lot. It pulled in front of the hospital, right up on the curb; and damn near ran over the people standing there on the sidewalk. After it came to a stop, they rolled this motherfucker out the back on a stretcher."

"Who is you talking bout B?"

"Your boy Taps. That nigga looked like he was fucking dead when they brought him in."

"Yo B I don't fuck with that nigga like that. He ain't my boy."

"Word? It's like that? I thought you niggas was tight and shit. Ha, that's funny, but yo check this out, his moms and pops showed up in a whole different ambulance. They were fucked up too. Black eyes, bruises, all types of crazy shit. My G, they even had a priest there praying over him. They were going all out for this nigga."

His homeboy interjected,

"A rabbi motherfucker, that was a rabbi. Jewish motherfuckers don't fuck with priests... Right Robert?"

"Right... This nigga don't know what the

fuck he talking about. Get your facts straight B… Is that nigga dead or what?"

"Nah, he's still kicking as far as I know. My moms is off today, but when she goes back I'll get her to find out."

"It's not that serious B, I don't give a fuck either way."

I kicked it with them for a little bit longer, dapped them up and then said my goodbyes; all the while thinking damn, Manuel didn't get the job done.

As I was walking off, the main nigga that was doing all the talking, called out my name.

"Yo Rob, hold up!"

He slowly jogged over and caught up with me; his man trailed behind. Together we walked along and continued on with the same bullshit conversation, but something wasn't quite right. He started to get a little bit too friendly, and placed his arm around my shoulder while we walked.

"Rob man, I just want you to know that you're a cool dude, and I don't want you to take what we're about to do to you personal. But word on the street is, it's open season on your ass. Niggas is paying niggas to fuck you up, and we can't miss out on getting this paper."

Before I had a chance to figure out what was going on, or have a chance to react, I felt a sharp pain in my stomach. I looked down and saw him pull some type of blade straight out of my gut, and stick it right back in. He repeated the motion several more times, while his boy grabbed me from behind and tried to keep me from moving.

He grunted every time he swung the blade, right then I knew he was trying to inflict some real harm. After the initial first few strikes, my hands started to take the brunt of the damage. I blocked, twisted, turned, and tried my best to get away. Some how I ended up on the ground, and despite the fact that all of this was happening in broad daylight, not that I was expecting it, but no one tried to stop it. People walked by and straight up ignored it.

This obviously wasn't planned. I walked right into it and they seized the opportunity. I couldn't be mad, because I probably would have done the same thing. I just wish I knew who was behind it, and why. The only thing I did know was that they succeeded. It was over for me, a done deal... At least I thought.

The slow beeping of a heart monitor was the first thing I heard when I came to. The light in the room was blinding my eyes, and the smell of cheap perfume was killing my nose. My first thought was dam, I must be in the hospital. Besides Tiffany and my mom, West Indian women are the only women I've been around that wear that brand of cheap perfume; and that's all who work in this hospital.

My arms were strapped down to the bed, they had a tube stuck in my dick, and a bunch of wires attached to my arm. All I heard in the background was my mom yucking it up with one of the doctors or a nurse. Somebody eventually shut the door to my room and canceled out all the outside noise.

As I laid there staring up at the ceiling I thought, wow, another close call. I'm in pain but I'm still alive. I'll be back on my feet in no time, and all those who had something to do with this will have hell to pay.

I took a deep breath, closed my eyes, and tried my best to relax; but for some strange reason I couldn't get comfortable. It felt like there was a presence in the room. That smell of cheap perfume became overwhelming. I opened my eyes again to see if anyone could have slipped in unannounced, and momentarily caught a glimpse of someone's face. Then everything went black.

They had put a pillow over my head and was holding it down tight, smothering me. I squirmed and flailed around a bit, kicked my feet, but it was to no avail. I gasped for air. I coughed, I gasped, I, I was gone…

18 "IF YOU WANT SOMETHING SAID, ASK A MAN; IF YOU WANT SOMETHING DONE, ASK A WOMAN." - MARGARET THATCHER

"He was a troubled young man, but he had a good heart. He loved his momma; Lord knows he did. God had to bring him home!… Yes Jesus!… He had to bring him home and erase all the pain that was in his heart!… Yes lord! The pain was too great for such a young man to bare, that's why he had to call him home!… Praise God!"

Pastor Benjamin preached for a solid hour at Robert's funeral. He sure had a lot to say about someone he didn't know, but it was appreciated. The church was packed. Everyone came out for my baby. All his so-called friends and even family members who I haven't seen or heard from in years showed up. I was pleasantly surprised.

I know Robert would have loved it. He would've loved to have seen everyone together, but he would've been very disappointed seeing me there with Milford; cause he absolutely hated him.

I'm a little ashamed to admit this, but Milford and I kinda re-connected.

Yes, we're back together and I really don't owe anyone an explanation, including Robert, but I'll try to explain.

You see, Milford stepped up in my time of need and got me through a tough situation. We temporarily put all our bullshit aside and came together for this tragedy; no matter how fucked up it may look. I did what I had to do for me, and not for anyone else.

At the funeral I couldn't stop rocking back and forth in the pew. It looked as if I was trying to dodge the streams of light that was shining through the stained glass windows, but it was my nerves making me rock like that. I guess it was a coping mechanism for all the pain and guilt I was feeling; maybe it was a little more guilt, than pain.

I couldn't stop the tears from rolling down my cheeks as the preacher prayed, and even though I tried, it was hard to contain my screams during certain parts of the prayer. Some of his words would hit me so hard that I couldn't control myself.

My nose was running, and so was my mascara. I had black streak marks from my eyes to my chin. I was a complete mess.

Milford and my mom tried to console me, but with all my sobbing, rocking back and forth, and the not so private conversations that I was having with myself; I was damn near inconsolable.

"Robert, I know you're probably up in heaven looking down on me, angry, and shaking your head; you have every right to be, but please don't be. I have enough people looking at me crazy right now. My only wish is that you could be here in person, not in spirit, to see the massive turnout you got. I bet all would be forgiven. You wouldn't care about none of that bullshit with me or Milford."

I swear when I looked around the room I saw everyone from his middle school teacher to the dope boy on the block. My baby was loved. The only person that I felt some type of way about being there, was Taps. I would have never guessed that that boy would have shown his face up in there after all he done. He brought his parents along too. The nerve of that little dirty motherfucker; and to have Robert's daddy sitting over there next to him didn't make me feel any better. His stupid ass was supposed to have sat with the family.

They chatted back and forth the entire service, and I found it odd that they kept looking over at me. But I never turned away. I stared right back at them. I wanted to make them feel just as uncomfortable.

Even before the service started, Ivan, Robert's dad, was fully examining Robert's coffin like he was some type of coffin aficionado. He made it seem like I cut corners to save a buck, and even commented on how he didn't like the way Robert was dressed. It was all I could do not to go off on that cheap ass motherfucker. He didn't pay one dime toward the funeral, never paid any child support, he ain't never do shit but complain about how I was raising my son. Now he wants to sit next to that little bastard and talk about me. I couldn't wait till the service was over so I could lay into his ass.

My mom, who is scared to fly but flew here from L.A., just to bury her grandson, grabbed my hand and gave me a look like, 'please don't start no mess up in here; this is the house of the Lord'. Out of respect for her, I chilled out for the time being, but the moment we got outside it was on.

At first I was gonna walk up to him and just curse his ass out, but by the time the service was over I had simmered down a bit, and figured that a cooler head would probably prevail. I tried to make a conscious effort to put all the ghetto shit behind me for the sake of Robert. But I still wasn't about to let Ivan slide. I just went about it a little different. I pulled him to the side, and calmly tried to explain how I didn't appreciate his actions that day. But being the thick headed Russian that he is; he dismissed it. That's when I went off. I didn't care who was around. He needed to eat everything I was serving, and I was serving up a lot. Most of the attendees stood to the side and let me do my thing; all except one. Taps mom. With her finger in front of her lips, she stuck her flat ass between us and tried to shush me, as if I was a little kid. Milford must have saw it coming, because he caught my hand midway and stopped it from slapping the taste out that raggedy bitch's mouth.

After Robert was laid to rest, everyone went their separate ways. Only a couple of close friends and a few family members came by the house. Ivan wasn't one of them. He actually left with Taps and his family. I have to say, I wasn't too surprised. Maybe it's a white thing, but it seemed like they instantly bonded as soon as they met. I thought that they were only gonna give him a ride to the hotel or airport, so his cheap ass wouldn't have to pay for a cab. I Later found out that he went back to their house for dinner, spent the night there, and flew back to wherever the fuck he came from the next morning. What a sorry man he is.

19 "MISTAKES ARE ALWAYS FORGIVABLE, IF ONE HAS THE COURAGE TO ADMIT THEM". - BRUCE LEE

'Why'd you do it mama? Did you want to be with him that bad? I was planning on leaving; you didn't have to kill me.'

"Would you please stop saying that Robert? I would never hurt you. I only want the best for you, you know that. Stop accusing me of shit I didn't do!"

'But you were right outside of the room mama. How could have this have happened with you standing right there, unless you had something to do with it?'

"Well I'm telling you that I didn't Robert, what do I have to do to make you believe me? How could you even think that I would do something like that?"

The back and forth between us went on for a good while, and it was starting to get heated. It wasn't until Milford shook me awake and called my name that I realized that it was all a dream.

"Charlene, Charlene, wake up your having another nightmare."

I'd been having these dreams since the funeral, and by then he'd been buried for over two weeks. Every night it had gotten progressively worse, and with the limited sleep that I was getting, it made it hard for me to function during the day. On top of that, I began to drink excessively. I was back to smoking cigarettes again, and I also started dabbling in drugs.

I got high off of anything and everything I could get my hands on, but nothing seemed to ease the pain.

I admit, in the past there were times when I wished that Robert was gone. It was out of my frustration with him from all the trouble that he'd been getting into. I feel terrible about it now, I know I can't take it back, and I'm trying to deal with the guilt.

Not to mention, I should've listened to him and completely cut my ties with Milford when I had the chance. I know I said that we worked things out and that we were back together, but I think I made a mistake. A real big mistake.

He was slowly getting back on his bullshit; meaning, he was back to being over bearing and possessive. It'll only be a matter of time before we're physically fighting again; I just know it.

He was cool the whole time leading up to the funeral, and for a short time thereafter; but starting from the day my mom was set to return home, things began to go downhill.

She had been staying with us for a couple of days after the funeral, and that was a real comfort for me; but Milford didn't see it like that. If he had it his way, she would've been on the plane as soon as Robert's coffin hit the dirt; and he made sure that he let it be known. Some of the slick comments he made caused us to have a full blown argument right in front of her. We both said some fucked up shit, but certain things that he said, led me to believe that all his past boo hooing and apologizing wasn't sincere at all.

Despite all the negative vibes I was getting from him, I stayed. I continued to take his verbal abuse day in and day out, and it was starting to effect me. I ended up having to bite my tongue a lot of the time so things wouldn't escalate. Without my mom or Robert around; I felt that no one else had my back.

Oddly enough, I still had one person who I thought I had in my corner, and that was Tiffany.

We had hashed things out a while ago, and kinda sorta rekindled our friendship, and in the last couple of weeks we'd become super tight. After being hit with tragedy after tragedy, I'm glad that we had each other's shoulder to cry on.

She'd been coming by the house everyday since Robert passed; I only wish that I've could have been a better friend to her when she was dealing with the death of Keke.

Her relationship with Milford even did a 360. He used to couldn't stand her, but now all of a sudden they're cool. In fact I think they would consider themselves friends.

A couple of times I came home and she was there hanging out with him on the couch; laughing, joking, and having a good old time. I was a little surprised, but wasn't bothered by it. After she left, I tried to joke about it with him, but he didn't find it funny. All I said was that they looked like lovebirds; and that nigga went crazy. He started calling me out my name, saying disrespectful things about Robert, and made threats.

I told Tiffany about it the next day, and she was neither here or there. If I were to bet though, I'd say she was leaning more toward his side. Her silence said a lot.

In hindsight, I should have known better than to open up and make myself vulnerable to someone that I previously had a major beef with. The trust could never be 100%. I let the grief overwhelm me, and the weed smoke keep me in a fog. If I would've paid more attention, and didn't care so much about getting high, I would've seen that something wasn't quite right.

My vices were starting to get out of control. I was still able to maintain somewhat of a daily routine, and function at work as if everything was normal, but behind closed doors I had to get my smoke on, my drink on, or both.

One day on my way home from work I slid by Tiffany's place, not necessarily to see her, but to buy some weed. There are like a million drug dealers that hang out outside her building, and they be battling each other for customers. I had become a regular in recent weeks, so they knew what I was there for without me having to ask.

While I was negotiating my transaction, I noticed this old raggedy Jaguar pull into the parking lot. The car looked vaguely familiar but I couldn't place it at the time. To be honest my head was some where else. But then I saw Tiff run out the building and hop in it, and that immediately got my attention. I took my hand, rubbed my eyes, and stared a little harder to see who it was that she got in the car with, and realized that it was Taps. I thought to myself, what the hell is going on here? Why is she chopping it up with this motherfucker? I didn't even think she knew him.

She chatted with him for a few minutes, then got out, and he drove off. From that point on, all the getting high shit got temporarily put on hold. I had to find out what was going on. Not only for myself but for Robert.

I didn't wait. I immediately threw the money at the boy who was selling me the weed, snatched the sack out his hand, and quickly rolled up my window. Then I slid down low in the seat, and hoped that she wouldn't see me, or recognize my car. But as fate would have it, right when she was about to open the door to her building, she spotted me.

After doing a double take, she called out my name, then slowly started to walk over to my vehicle. I tried to play it off like I was looking for something in the glove compartment, and waited until she got to the driver's side door and tapped on the window, before I rolled it down to acknowledge her.

Acting like I was surprised I said,

"Tiffany, girl you scared the shit out of me. I didn't even see you out here."

"I was just heading back inside," she replied. "Why didn't you tell me that you were coming by? Did you call? Cause I left my phone upstairs and might have missed it."

"No I didn't call. I only came by to buy some weed. I didn't think you'd be home."

"Oh, okay…"

Tiffany stood there and stared at me for a good minute, like she was waiting for me to say something about her and Taps, but I didn't. We continued on with the small talk, while I shared a blunt with her, then we said our goodbyes. I don't know why, but she waited until I pulled off before she went back inside. She normally didn't do that.

It took me a whole 10 minutes give or take to drive home, and I guess Milford wasn't expecting me. I walked in on him having an intense conversation with someone on the phone, and he quickly tried to hang up.

"Let me go. She just came through the door. I'll holla at you later," he whispered.

"Did I interrupt something?"

"Nah, that was just one of my homeboys from work."

He began to stare at me the same way Tiffany did. I guess he was expecting me to get all bent out of shape or press him about who he was talking to on the phone; but I didn't. I was chill. I knew that I would find out soon enough anyway.

When his stupid ass jumped up to use the bathroom, he forgot and left his phone on the kitchen table. I picked it up and checked the call log to see who the last caller was, and bingo, my suspicions were confirmed. It was Tiffany.

They're somehow in cahoots with each other. How Taps fits in to this I had yet to figure out, but I know they're up to something. If I find out that they had anything at all to do with what happened to Robert, oh God, I can't even say what I would do.

The police claim that the investigation into his death is still ongoing, but I haven't received a single update on the case. Whenever I try to talk to Milford about it, he gets annoyed, and it ends up turning into a big argument. He's always quick to say, "you ain't a cop, let them motherfucker's do they job," and it escalates from there. But I never let his negative comments deter me, I'm constantly searching for answers. Every time I play it out in my head, I'm always asking myself, what am I missing?

I arrived at the hospital shortly after Robert was admitted. He had a successful surgery, and I was at his bedside when he came to. He was absolutely fine. Later they informed me that he passed away in his sleep, but no one can give me a solid reason why. All they can tell me is that it looked like it was foul play.

What's hard to understand is how could this have happened when the only people allowed in the room besides the detectives investigating his assault, was a doctor and a couple of nurses.

What's also strange is that he laid there dead for 8 hours before anyone realized that he was gone. Everyone claimed that they thought he was asleep.

I know I have a lawsuit, but I don't care about that. I just want to know who killed my son.

20 "KNOWLEDGE IS OF NO VALUE UNLESS YOU PUT IT INTO PRACTICE." - ANTON CHEKHOV

For the first time in weeks, I didn't wake up from a bad dream. I started my day without a hangover, and I was laser focused on seeking out answers. Just looking at Milford's sloppy ass was turning my stomach. I was now seeing him with sober eyes, and it showed me how much of a fool I've been. But I couldn't let my new view of him be revealed. I had to continue to act how I would normally act; I didn't want him to suspect a thing.

My plan was to meet with his mother. Something that under any normal circumstance I'd never consider doing. It's not a secret; everyone knows I can't stand that bitch, I just desperately need to get some information from her.

I was trying to figure out what I could say or do to prevent her from going back and telling him; because that woman can't keep her mouth shut to save her life.

In my frivolous attempt to keep things under wrap, I told her that I was planning on throwing him a surprise birthday party, and that I would like her to help me with it. Despite his birthday being over six months away, she didn't question it, and she also promised to keep our little secret.

From the day Milford got out of jail, I've been wondering how she got the money to bail him out. She barely had two nickels to rub together, yet alone knew someone who would lend her any cash. She wasn't well liked in the neighborhood, and would be hard pressed to even borrow a cup of sugar. I knew if we chatted long enough she would eventually tell me how she got it, but I didn't have all day. I had to cleverly weave in the questions I wanted answered without her realizing what I was trying to do. So while chit chatting about what kind of cake to get, and who should be invited to the party, I was able to sneak a couple of my questions in.

She told me that one of Milford's friends,

a short chubby chick with blonde hair, reached out to her looking to help. The woman gave her the money, even took her down to the bail bonds office, and she claimed that it all happened out of the blue. Right off the bat I knew that it was Tiffany she was talking about. I just couldn't figure out why she would do it, or even how she was able to come up with the money. Tiffany is just as broke if not broker than Milford's mom; but she's a schemer, and I wouldn't put nothing past her.

I remember how she was when Robert got out of jail. How she was feening to know who it was that he was ranting and raving about. On that day, Robert was praising Taps like there was no tomorrow. Talking about all the money his family had, the neighborhood he lived in, yada yada yada, just a whole bunch of nonsense. Tiffany was all ears, and she apparently took notes; I assume that's what led to their meeting outside of her building. Knowing the little bit I know about Taps, I can only guess he was there to discuss how she was planning to pay him back.

Tiffany, undoubtedly, totally, and willingly betrayed me.

Now I see why Milford suddenly became so cool with her. And to think, I thought he was just trying to fuck; but he was kissing her ass, all because she bailed him out.

Within 20 minutes of meeting Milford's mom, I got most of my questions answered; but I spent hours trying to get rid of this bitch. She wanted to talk and talk about the stuff she did way back in 1978, and I wasn't trying to hear that shit.

I was coming up with excuse after excuse on why I had to leave, but couldn't convince this woman to let me go. She was so needy, and I was trying real hard not to be disrespectful. I was right at my breaking point when she suddenly jumped up and asked me what time it was. After I told her, she said she had to leave because she couldn't miss Judge Mathis. Would you believe that shit?

I had to sit in my car for a while after that, just to decompress. I was trying to come up with a plan of action before I headed home. I couldn't walk in that door and look that fat motherfucker in his face and continue to pretend like everything was ok.

I was almost certain Milford had something to do with Roberts death, but I didn't have evidence to go to the police. Most of what I had was speculation and gut feelings. I needed something more substantial.

When I arrived home later that evening, I was trying to decide whether or not to go in. All the lights were on in the house, the shades were up, and I could see Milford's big ass sitting on the couch from the street. I had butterflies in my stomach. It had to be the most nervous feeling I've felt since I've been with him. It got worse when I saw Tiffany walk pass the window. Her being there now took on a whole new meaning. I knew they were plotting something, and I wasn't gonna walk right into it. I put the keys back in the ignition and was about to turn it, when someone tapped on my drivers side window. I damn near shit on myself.

It was a middle aged woman sporting long dreadlocks with sea shells attached to them; and she was dressed in light blue colored scrubs. I never saw this woman before in my life, but she seemed to be just as nervous as I was. For all I know she could've been one of Milford's cronies, so I only cracked my window a little bit to hear what she had to say. Speaking with a thick

West Indian accent she asked,

"Miss, can I chat with you for a minute?"

I reciprocated with a head nod, and she continued to talk.

"It's about your son my sister. I think I may have some information for you."

She wrote something down on a small piece of paper, folded it, and slid it through the window.

Only thing written on it was the name of a doctor. Doctor Irving Singer.

I didn't know who the hell he was, and when I turned to ask the woman, she was gone.

Just like that, she disappeared, vanished. I stepped out of the car, looked in both directions, up and down the street, but there was no sign of her.

While debating on what to do next, I spotted Milford standing in the doorway of the house watching me.

"What's up Charlene? What you looking for?" He shouted.

I was stumped for a hot second, but quickly pulled myself together and replied,

"Oh, nothing. It's such a beautiful evening; I was just trying to take it all in."

He backed up against the storm door and

held it wide open, and motioned for me to come inside. As I passed, he leaned in for a kiss and I reluctantly gave him a peck on the lips. I only did it because I didn't want him to think that anything was wrong.

Tiffany was posted up on the couch, nursing what looked to be a half of glass of Hennessey. She wasn't really drinking it; just shaking it around in the ice.

"What's going on Charlene? What you fin to get into tonight?" She asked.

"Nothing girl. I think I'm gonna turn in early. I got some shit I need to get done at work tomorrow."

"Come on Charlene, what they got you doing that's so important that you have to go to bed before 8:00? You work at Red Lobster. They don't even open till 11am."

Milford chuckled before he cut her off and interjected with a question of his own.

"I see you already made friends with the new neighbor. What was she talking about?"

"New neighbor? What new neighbor?"

"The lady you were just talking to out front; that moved in the house across the street."

I tried to play it off.

"Oh, that lady. She wanted to know what day was garbage day."

Everything else Milford and Tiffany said that evening went in one ear and right out the other. My mind was focused on the new neighbor. I couldn't wait to speak to her again.

I could barely sleep at all that night, and got up first thing the next morning hoping to catch her before she left for work. I really didn't know her schedule, and felt that it was way too early to go and knock on her door. So I waited, and waited, and waited, until I couldn't wait no more. I quietly slipped out the house and went over to her residence.

Knock knock knock.

"Hello is anybody home? It's the neighbor from across the street. I spoke with you yesterday evening. Ma'am are you home?"

I knocked on the door a few more times but no one answered. I was about ready to give up, when the sound of Milford's voice scared the ever living crap out of me.

"Charlene! Why are you banging on this lady's door this time of morning? What the hell is wrong with you?"

I quickly turned around to face him and replied,

"There ain't nothing wrong with me. What the fuck is wrong with you? Why are you sneaking around behind me?"

"Ain't nobody sneaking behind you. You out here making all this noise first thing in the morning. Waking up the neighborhood. Take your ass back home!"

Things were about to get real ugly. I began to load up my mental arsenal and was preparing to explode on this motherfucker.

Suddenly a car slowly pulled into the driveway. It was the neighbor, and she looked nervous. I can't blame her, I would be to if I rolled up on two strangers standing in my yard screaming at each other 6:00 in the morning.

Talk about being embarrassed, Milford was too, and he took his fat ass back across the street.

I stood there and waited for her to get out the car.

"Is everything alright?" she asked.

I shook my head yes, and~handed her back the paper that she gave me from yesterday.

"Who is this doctor and what does he

have to do with my son?" I asked.

The woman looked back toward my house as if she were checking to see if Milford was gone before she responded.

"Come, lets talk inside." She said.

I wasn't there for a social visit, and refused to sit down after she offered me a seat. I stood in her living room with my arms folded in front of me, waiting for the answer.

"Okay I'll get right to the point; Dr Singer is a prominent staff member at the hospital where I work, and where your son was admitted. He wasn't treating your son, but I saw him go in and out of his room a few times that day," she explained.

"Okay, so, so what?… What's wrong with that?"

"There's nothing wrong with it, but I overheard him talking about your son with a relative of his, who was also a patient there at the time."

"Well what did he say?"

"I really didn't get the gist of the conversation. All I heard was the Doctor mentioning your son's name, and saying he'll take care of him."

"Ma'am that could of been anything. No

offense, but I thought you had some real information for me; not this bullshit."

I felt like this whole thing was just a waste of time, and I started to head out her front door.

"Sammy Singer!" She shouted.

"What?"

"Sammy Singer. His name is Sammy Singer. He's the Doctor's grandson. The kids in the neighborhood call him Taps. That's who the Doctor was talking to."

21 "OUR LIVES BEGIN TO END THE DAY WE BECOME SILENT ABOUT THINGS THAT MATTER." - MARTIN LUTHER KING JR.

Now that the woman had my full attention, I stayed back to listen to more of what she had to say. She began by telling me that her name was Priscilla, and that she worked as a nurses aid at the hospital. I didn't want to come off as being rude, but there was no need for her to tell me her back story, I just wanted her to get to the point. I politely spun my hand repeatedly to speed her along, because I was starting to become more and more impatient.

She finally went on to explain that not only did she see Dr Singer go in and out of Robert's room; she claimed that there's a video of it.

The hospital had security cameras

everywhere; but it wouldn't do me any good if none of them showed what went on in the room. They were only setup at the entrances and exits of the building, and in the hallways; so it would have been impossible to point the finger at one particular person based on the amount of traffic going in and out of that room that day. I'm not a detective, but that video alone, and me trying to explain to the cops what happened wouldn't be enough. This woman would have to come down to the police station with me and make a statement.

She refused.

Naturally I was upset, but I shouldn't have expected her to do any more. When you're from the hood, running to the police to solve your problems is frowned upon. So I can understand her reservations; but this was my child that we were talking about. I would have thought she'd have some compassion. Her not wanting to talk to the police left me frustrated.

I returned home with all of that shit weighing on my mind, and completely forgot that moments earlier I had been beefing with Milford. And for him, our disagreement was far from being over. He was still feeling some type of way about it.

I walked through the door of my home with my guard down, and was completely blindsided. He slapped me across my face so hard that it made my ears ring.

It was like he couldn't wait to put his hands on me again. All he needed was a good reason, and this was it.

When I tried to get away, he stuck out his foot and tripped me, and I tumbled head first to the floor.

He continued to stomp and kick me, and wouldn't let up no matter how loud I screamed. The last thing I remember was him choking me, until I passed out. I don't know for how long, It may have only been for a few minutes, but when I came to; I was a mess. My fingernails were broken, a patch of my hair was pulled out, and the robe I was wearing had drops of my blood running down the front of it.

Milford was sitting on the couch watching tv and eating a bowl of cereal; acting like nothing ever happened. He even had the nerve to try and strike up a conversation after everything he did to me.

"Charlene, some of the fellas might stop by later to watch the game; once you get yourself together, I need you to run to the store and pick up some soda and chips," he said.

Right then I realized that this had to end today, and now would be the perfect time to end it.

My eyes were fixated on the back of his big ass head as I pushed myself up from off of the floor.

I started looking around for something that I could use as a weapon, and decided to go with what I already had in my possession. The belt from my robe.

I slowly pulled it through the robe one loop after another, until I had it free. I stretched it out and wrapped each end tightly around both of my hands; making sure that I had a good grip.

I quietly scooted across the floor while on my knees, until I was right behind him. I got so close I was scared that he would feel my breath on the back of his neck, but he was too preoccupied by the T.V. to even notice.

He was so busy chuckling at whatever he was watching, that he was totally unaware of me.

Then I did it.

I sprung up, wrapped the belt around his

throat, and dropped to the floor. I used all 120 pounds of me to hold his neck down over the top back edge of the couch, but feared that it might not be enough. In his attempt to free himself, he grabbed the belt, leaned forward, and tried his best to stand up. He was starting to lift me. My knees were sliding around on the floor, and he was gurgling and slinging his spit everywhere. Even though my arms and hands were beginning to hurt, I refused to let go. It wasn't long before he stopped struggling, and fell back onto the couch. I could actually feel the life leave his body.

All the rage that I was feeling inside made me hold on considerably longer than I should have, because I was still choking him way after he stopped moving. I didn't even realize that Priscilla had knocked on the door, let herself in, and was watching me as I strangled him to death.

It wasn't until we locked eyes, that I let him go.

Whatever the reason for her visit, she changed her mind quick. She saw what was going on and began to moonwalk back out of the door. The bitch hauled ass before I had the chance to explain to her what happened.

Later I found out the reason for her coming over was because she had a change of heart. She was willing to go with me to the police, and tell them everything she knew.

She still ended up going down there to talk to them, but it wasn't to give them information about the death of Robert, or tell them what she knew about Doctor Singer or Taps; it was to tell them everything that she saw, and knew about me.